the forever vow

A BILLIONAIRE ARRANGED-MARRIAGE ROMANCE

THE FOREVER SERIES
BOOK 3

LEIGH JAMES

GEMINI PRESS

The Forever Vow

A Billionaire Arranged Marriage Romance

Copyright © 2022 by Leigh James.

Published by Gemini Press.

dedication

This book is for everyone who is trying to be a good person. Are you out there trying to do the right thing, even when no one else is watching?

It can be hard. The world can be hard.

But you are making it a better place for all of us—do not give up on yourself. Do not give up on the idea that your goodness, your kindness, can make a difference in the world. Do not give up on hope.

Xoxo, Leigh

ONE

damages

CHLOE

IT WAS CERTAINLY NOT the letter I'd been hoping for. *Hey Chloe,* texted Elena, the madam who'd hired me. *Bryce's attorney hand-delivered a message this morning. You better read this ASAP.*

I sighed as I re-read the attachment.

Dear Mrs. Windsor:
Your husband, Bryce Windsor, has retained us as counsel. I have attached a copy of your post-nuptial contract for your records.

Please be advised that pursuant to Section 72-F of your agreement, you are hereby in default. Our client is exercising his right to demand specific performance of the contract terms within forty-eight (48) hours from today. Failure to perform constitutes a breach on your part, which will result in our client seeking damages, up to and including punitive ones.

An associate from our office will be following up shortly.

Sincerely,
Jim Wright, Senior Partner
Kellogg, Kramer and Wright LLP

My phone buzzed—my attorney, Akira Zhang, was calling again. I'd already sent her to voicemail three times, but she didn't give up easily. "Hey, Akira."

"What the *fuck*, Chloe?" she hollered into my ear. "Jim Wright *hand-delivered* a letter to Accommo-Dating this morning! Do you know what he charges? Three thousand dollars an *hour*! Elena said he freaking walked there! That's a fifteen-hundred dollar walk."

"So what?" I asked, careful to keep my voice down. My younger brother, Noah, was asleep in the bed next to mine. "Bryce can afford it." My estranged husband, Bryce Windsor, was a billionaire. His family was one of the wealthiest in the United States. If anyone could afford three thousand dollars an hour, it was Bryce.

"You don't get it. Bryce is coming after you hard." She sounded agitated. "His law firm mentioned *punitive* damages. Do you know what that means?"

"No."

"It means he's going to sue you for everything you've got! And he's going to sue Elena, AccommoDating, and probably me because he's pissed and has piles of money to burn. It means you need to go back to the island and finish your contract within forty-eight hours —or you're screwed."

Bryce was my husband, but our marriage was hardly traditional. We'd signed a contract before we wed. He paid me money—lots of it—to be his bride. Things had been great for a while...until he fired me.

Bryce had offered me another contract for even more money if I agreed to return. I accepted, but things had gone wrong. Terribly wrong. So I'd left him, and now everything was a mess. He was threatening to sue me, I was hiding in a crappy motel with my brother, and Akira Zhang was yelling at me to go back to my husband.

But I couldn't. And I couldn't tell her why.

I swallowed hard. "I thought you said you could help me," I reminded her. "You said you could get me out of this if I wanted. Remember? Back when you were saying this was a messed-up arrangement?"

"Oh, I remember." Akira's voice rose. "Do *you* remember that I told you this contract was—if I recall my words correctly—some 'seriously fucked-up shit?'"

"Yes." If only I'd listened to her.

"Can you tell me that Bryce did something bad?" Her tone turned hopeful. "Because if he hurt you or Noah, *we're* going to be the ones seeking damages. Just say the word."

I sighed. "He didn't do anything wrong." Except make me fall in love with him.

"Then why won't you go back?" she asked.

"I just... I don't want to. I can't."

Akira groaned, then stress-counseled me about breach of contract, Jim Wright's exorbitant hourly rate, and what might happen if I didn't return to my marriage. But I couldn't follow her words. All I could think about was Bryce. I shouldn't blame him for what happened—for how my heart was broken. Our wedding had been arranged. It was supposed to be contractual, strictly business. He paid me to say 'I do' because he needed to be married in order to vest in his family business. I'd eagerly taken the money. It was enough to change my life. It would've kept my brother safe for years, maybe for forever.

I glanced over at Noah, who was still sleeping. He

was *not* happy with me right now; I didn't blame him. So many things had changed since I'd married Bryce— my poor brother must have whiplash. We'd gone from living in a crappy motel to residing in an ocean-front mansion and then back again.

Earlier that summer, Bryce had fired me. Then he'd lured me back with the promise of even more money. We hadn't made it very far before we parted ways again. This time around, I was the one who'd broken things off. I'd run off with Noah in the middle of the night. We'd left our clothes, our friends, and Noah's new puppy.

I'd walked away from the money, too.

Not to mention my husband.

But in the end, it wasn't the dollars that mattered. It wasn't the promise of wealth that had undone me. It was Bryce himself. I'd fallen madly in love with him— not a smart thing for a girl from the wrong side of the tracks. And it was my love for him that forced me to break my contract.

"They're going to back you into a wall," Akira continued.

Boy, did I know how that felt.

Bryce's father, Gene Windsor, was the reason I'd left. He'd never approved of me. He wanted Bryce to marry his ex-girlfriend, Felicia Jones, an American heiress—or someone rich like her. Not someone like me, from the crappy part of East Boston, trash who came from trash. Gene had been very clear: he wanted me gone. He'd threatened me, he'd threatened Noah, and he'd threatened Bryce's position with the company if I didn't do what he asked, which was leave for good. Gene Windsor had ruined my chance at a happy life with the man I loved.

And now Bryce was about to sue me because he wanted me back. But Gene would hurt my brother *and* my husband if I returned. I couldn't tell anyone the truth. Gene would come after me if I did.

So what the hell was I supposed to do?

"What if I say no?" I interrupted Akira's tirade. "What happens if I refuse to go back?" I needed to make a decision quick.

"They'll probably file an emergency motion seeking injunctive relief. The way the contract is set up, there would be a private arbitration process."

"Can you say that in English, please?" Akira's lawyer-speak was sometimes over my head.

She sighed. "Injunctive relief means they'll ask an arbiter—a private judge—to make you perform the contract."

"And what if I refuse?"

6

"They'll ask that you pay contractual damages. And if you can't pay them, you might have to go to jail."

"Seriously?" I glanced over at my brother, who was blissfully asleep. If I went to jail, he would have no one except my father and my drunk-ass stepmother. Which was almost worse than no one...

"It's a stretch to ask for jail time in a private matter, but we're talking about a lot of money. And the Windsors have a crap-ton of political connections. They make donations. They have everything stacked in their favor."

"So what do I do?"

Akira was quiet for a minute. Probably her brain was going into overdrive, making assessments and calculations. "You should meet with Jim Wright. Tell him that you're willing to listen."

"Can you be on the call, too?" I asked.

"Of course, Chloe. I'll be with you every step of the way." But she made it sound like we might be walking the plank. "I'll reach out to him and set up a meeting. My guess is he'll want to do it soon—Bryce is probably his biggest client."

I sighed again. "Of course he is."

"You might want to call Elena when you have a second," Akira said. "She's kind of freaking out."

"Ugh."

"Ugh is the nice word for it." Akira hung up.

I sighed and texted Elena. *Can you talk?*

My phone immediately rang.

"Please tell me you're going to make this right." Elena blew out a deep breath. "I can't deplete my girls' college funds because of a lawsuit. Do you know how much college *costs* these days?"

"No, I don't." Continuing education wasn't exactly part of my life plan after my mother died. "And I'm sorry for the trouble."

"Listen, I know this has been a difficult assignment," the madam said. "It was a big ask, having you marry someone sight-unseen and packing you off to live with him on a remote island. But the thing is, Chloe, you did it. You made it work. So why now? You still haven't told me what happened."

"It's complicated."

"I know you got drunk and got into a fight at Caroline Vale's wedding. That's not like you, Chloe. I thought you'd never had a drink."

"I hadn't. Not until that night. Then I had three shots of tequila." I grimaced—it hadn't been my finest hour.

"What were you thinking?" Elena sounded more like a mother than a madam. "And the fight with Felicia. The pictures are God-awful!"

I winced. The most famous shot was of me on top of

Felicia Jones, straddling her, my teeth bared as I pulled her hair. I'd been wearing that revealing red dress, the one Gene Windsor had picked out. The fight had been his idea; he'd wanted me to publicly humiliate myself.

"I was upset," I said. "She was still texting Bryce. She was nasty to me. So I got drunk and did something stupid. You can understand that, can't you?"

"Sure," Elena said, surprising me. "Sometimes you have to tell people to back off. But that doesn't explain why you left. You must have real feelings for Bryce if she got under your skin. So why leave? And we both know you desperately need the money."

"I left because I *do* have real feelings for him, Elena." I sucked at lying, so it was best to stick as close to the truth as possible. "That's why. I embarrassed him. His family won't ever accept me. And now he's going to be acting CEO of the company, and with his father's trial coming up, Bryce is going to be all over the media. I can't drag him down like that."

"I understand what you're saying, but there's an important piece to this that you're not acknowledging."

"What's that?"

"*Him,*" she said. "He wants you back, Chloe. There are always two people in a marriage, even one that's arranged. You can't forget that he's his own person and capable of making decisions for himself. Don't take that away from him. If you want to leave for *you*—because this isn't what you want and you can't do it anymore—fine. Pay the damages, go to jail, drain my girls' college funds, whatever. I will support you if that's what you really want. But if you're not going back because you think you know what's best for him, check yourself."

She went quiet for a moment. "Bryce Windsor is his own man. So let him make his choice. And you need to make yours. Call me when you decide, okay? I'll probably be busy moving my assets to an off-shore account, but I'll always take your call."

"Ha," I said, but I had a sinking feeling she wasn't kidding. "I'll think about it, okay?"

"Okay, Chloe."

But when she hung up, I knew the truth: nothing was okay.

Bryce Windsor is his own man. That was also the truth.

But where did that leave me?

injunctive relief

CHLOE

"Jim will be on the call momentarily." Jim Wright's assistant, an older man with black-framed glasses, clicked some buttons on his computer. "Please hold."

Jim Wright had booked us for a video conference that morning. I wished I had something nice to wear, but I was stuck in my one clean T-shirt. I checked my image on my phone's screen, fixing my damp, frizzy hair. The motel's window air-conditioning unit barely worked and was no match for the humid August weather.

Noah and I were hiding in Ellsworth, Maine, about a half-hour drive from Northeast Harbor—only a few miles away from Bryce. Still, it seemed like another country. Being back in a crappy motel room after living in an oceanfront estate was jarring. Even though I'd grown up poor, I'd gotten accustomed to having a luxurious shower, a rolling lawn, and plenty of food to eat. Now I was back to scraping for change for the laundry machines, listening to my neighbor's death-metal playlist in the middle of the night, and worrying about how the hell I was going to get Noah his next meal.

They say money can't buy happiness, and that was the truth. But it could absolutely buy a lot of other shit!

Akira appeared on the screen, breaking my reverie. She wore her usual pink eyeglasses and high ponytail. "Hey, Chloe. Are we waiting for Attorney Wright?"

I nodded. "The assistant said he'd be right back."

Akira wrinkled her nose as she inspected me. "Are you in a *bathroom*?"

I sighed. "Noah's asleep in the bedroom. This is the only other space."

She started to say something, but Jim Wright appeared. He wore a golf shirt, and his skin was lightly tanned. "Hey there, it's Jim. Attorney Zhang, it's nice to meet you. Mrs. Windsor, you as well."

I mumbled a greeting, but Akira didn't bother with niceties. She got right to it. "My client's not interested in continuing with the contract," she said briskly. "She's looking to have it voided pursuant to section 81(b) for both duress and unconscionability. This agreement, on its face, is unconscionable. My client signed it under duress. At best, the terms are voidable. At worst, it's a major lawsuit waiting to happen. I'm sure *your* client wouldn't want another scandal—particularly one involving an escort agency."

Jim Wright didn't look impressed. "Attorney Zhang, I've heard such wonderful things about you. I'm surprised that you're opening with an empty threat. You counseled your client when she signed this, didn't you?"

Akira blinked at him. "I *tried* to counsel her—"

"Chloe is contractually forbidden from going public, even in a lawsuit, with the terms of this agreement." He sounded dead sure of himself. "I'm sure she doesn't want to lose guardianship rights to her brother. They're not exactly airtight, are they?"

Akira's gaze flicked to me. Bryce had paid off my father, bribing him to waive his parental rights to Noah. It wasn't exactly a legitimate agreement: I could easily lose Noah for good. He'd be sent back to my father and Lydia, returned to a life where he was taken for granted and mistreated. I couldn't let that happen, not ever.

"Akira..." My eyes filled with tears.

She sighed—she knew what I was thinking. She didn't need to hear more. "Go on," Akira told him.

"My client demands specific performance of the contract within forty-eight hours—just like my letter said." Jim Wright straightened his shoulders. "He's ready to send a car now. Chloe, what's your location?"

"I'm not telling you that." My mouth went dry. "I don't want to lose my brother, but I can't go back."

Jim watched me. "Can you tell me why?"

"No, I can't."

He tilted his chin. "Who are you protecting, Chloe?"

"N-No one." I could lose everything if I said one word about what Gene Windsor had threatened. I was backed up against a wall. There was no way out.

"Did my client harm you in any way?" He watched me carefully. "Physically or emotionally? Because if he did, this would turn into a different sort of conversation quickly. I'm not here to force you into anything harmful, Chloe."

"He didn't hurt me. Bryce would never do that." I raised my chin. It would be easy to lie, to claim that he'd harmed me in some way. Then I'd be free from the contract. Neither Jim Wright nor Akira would return me to a dangerous situation. Still, I wouldn't do that to Bryce. He'd never hurt me, and I wouldn't accuse him—not even to keep custody of my brother.

"If that's the case, I'm going to need you to say

more." Jim Wright was firm. "I need to understand your position."

"Well, actually..." I swallowed hard. "If I'm protecting anyone, it's Bryce. I got drunk at that wedding and attacked his ex-girlfriend. I embarrassed myself, and I embarrassed him. He's taking over as CEO of Windsor Enterprises—he can't exactly have me blowing his life up."

"My client said that behavior was very out of character for you."

"Does it matter?" I asked. "You've seen the headlines, haven't you? *Chloe Shows Her True Colors.* It's the truth. I don't belong in his world. He's a billionaire, and I'm nothing. It was too much for me—I blew it."

"I understand that you feel that way." Jim nodded. "But my client doesn't share that view. He believes it would be more detrimental for you two to split up than for you to continue."

An uncomfortable silence settled over the call.

"What are our options?" Akira asked.

"It's simple. Give me Chloe's address, and we'll send a car."

I shook my head. "I can't do that." Gene Windsor would have my head—or worse, Noah's.

"Fine. Jim nodded. "Then we'll set up an immediate hearing with a private arbiter. Chloe will be responsible for paying for half of the arbitration expenses, which will be costly. And we'll begin emergency proceedings in Massachusetts Family Court to have Noah returned to his actual legal guardian—his father."

My stomach plummeted. "No! You can't do that."

"I'm merely representing my client's best interests," Jim said smoothly.

Akira glared at him. "You pretend to be a nice guy, Jim. But you're an asshole."

"That might be true, but it's not going to get you out of this contract." He frowned. "I'm just doing my job, and you know it. So why don't you do yours? Speak with your client and give me an answer. I'll be on hold."

"Can they do that?" I asked as soon as his screen went blank. "Can they take Noah away from me?"

Akira sighed. "The agreement with your father won't stand up in court. Legally he's still Noah's guardian. I've started the process to change that, but it's a long one. And we don't have the kind of power that the Windsors have—they can do in days what could take us years. So right now, your guardianship *is* vulnerable. I'm surprised Bryce would threaten to do that, but he's playing hardball."

"I can't believe he'd do that to me."

Akira nodded. "It might not be him. Jim Wright is a known shark. He'll threaten anybody with anything, and he has no problem doing it. He looks like a regular middle-aged guy in his golf shirt, but he's lethal. That's why he's the best."

"But that means that I don't have much of a choice. Right?"

Akira shook her head. "You *always* have a choice, Chloe. It might get ugly if you decide to follow through on this, but if it's the right thing for you, I'll support you every step of the way. Bryce can outspend you, that's true. But that doesn't mean you have to stay married to him. If you want out, let's do this."

There was a knock on the door. "Chloe?" My brother sounded half-asleep. "There's someone outside. They want to talk to you."

"Don't open the door! Get in here." I yanked Noah inside the bathroom and handed him my phone. "Keep your eyes on Akira. Do not leave this room." I locked the bathroom behind me.

There was a knock on the motel room door. "Who is it?" My knees buckled.

"UPS. Package delivery," a man's voice said.

"Can you leave it outside?"

"You have to sign for it, ma'am. I'll step away from the door and leave the signature pad right outside. I'm not going to hurt you. Look out the window—you can see my truck in the lot."

I peered outside and was relieved to see a delivery truck pulled up in front of the motel. I opened the door a crack. The man, in a brown uniform, was already halfway down the hall. He held up his hands as though he were about to be arrested. "I have a daughter," he explained. "I tell her to never open the door for anybody, so I get it."

Touched, I quickly signed the electronic pad and slid the small package out from beneath it. "T-Thank you. Have a nice day." I closed the door immediately.

My hands were shaking as I looked at the padded envelope. The packing slip had my name and the motel room number on it. Who the hell knew where I was?

I opened it with shaking hands.

A key fob was inside with a BMW logo, along with a type-written note.

Chloe:
There's a car waiting outside for you. No driver. This has to be your choice.

Take Noah to the parking lot behind Main Street Market in Northeast. Dale will be waiting. Then use the navigation to drive to the Bar Harbor Airport.

I'm asking, Chloe. I won't come and drag you away like some kind of prisoner. If you aren't there within the hour, I'm telling my lawyers to follow the contract to the letter.

One hour. I'll receive a notification as soon as you sign for this, so the clock starts now.

I'll be there waiting. The rest is up to you.
- Bryce

Heart pounding, I peered out the window again. As the UPS truck drove away, a shiny silver BMW SUV appeared behind it. The car hadn't been in the lot this morning.

I clicked the key fob, and the SUV beeped.

Fuuck. What was I going to do? Maybe I could talk to Bryce, I reasoned. Perhaps I could tell him to his face that I couldn't come back, that we could never be together, and then beg him to let me keep Noah. My husband didn't have a hard heart toward me—at least, I prayed he didn't. Yet.

I burst back into the bathroom. "We have to go."

"What the heck's going on?" Akira said. "Jim Wright's waiting for us!"

"I know. But I have something I have to do—*now.* Tell Jim to call his client. He'll understand." I unceremoniously hung up the call and grabbed Noah. "Let's go, buddy. I'm taking you to meet Dale."

"Good." My brother wrenched himself out of my arms. "Maybe he'll have some food. Or my *dog*. Or anything that makes sense, unlike you."

I took a deep breath. "I probably deserve that." I *had* dragged the kid out of bed in the middle of the night and made him leave his puppy behind.

"Yeah, you do." Noah started stuffing his few belongings into his backpack, and I did the same.

We didn't have much time. I'd be cutting it close between the drive to Northeast and back to the airport. Plus, I *hated* driving. I hadn't been behind the wheel of a car since my mother died in an accident.

"How are we getting there?"

I held up the key. "Bryce left a car for us."

"At least I can depend on him." My brother stormed past me to the door, and I followed him out.

I stopped at the front desk to pay, but the lady shook her head. "It's been taken care of."

I nodded. "Thanks." But I wasn't sure that I meant it. Had Bryce known I was here all along? How? Had his men been watching me?

Did... Did his father know where we were?

That last question left me with a pit in my stomach as I unlocked the car and gingerly started it. Taking a deep breath, I left the relative safety of the motel lot. It had been a crappy place to stay, but for a brief moment, it had been an oasis.

Now I had to go and face my husband. I needed to deal with the ramifications of a lawsuit, the threat of losing my brother, and the possibility that Gene Windsor might find out and rain hellfire down on me. The crappy motel was looking better and better, but it was disappearing from my rearview mirror.

And I didn't know what lay ahead of me.

surprise

CHLOE

I RACED to Northeast Harbor to meet Dale, Bryce's assistant. He was accompanied by full security detail. After making him swear on his life that he'd keep my brother safe and on the mainland, I headed for the airport. I didn't trust many people, but Dale was one of the good guys. My brother loved him.

I still made Dale swear on his life. Twice.

I left the parking lot, the BMW roaring. The thing drove like a tank—I had a feeling that Bryce had selected it for that reason, that it would keep me safe. I carefully navigated back into the late-summer traffic, the navigation system guiding me down Route 198 to the airport. I drove below the speed limit the entire way, much to the chagrin of the line of traffic behind me.

As I passed the mountains and ocean views, my stomach somersaulted. I'd be seeing Bryce soon. What on earth was I going to say to him? I couldn't return to our marriage—I truly felt as though my hands were tied. Gene Windsor had seen to that. If I did, Gene would hurt my brother. He would hurt my husband.

I'd been ordered to stay away. I wanted what was best for Bryce—and of course, for my brother. But I couldn't help feeling a spark of hopefulness and excitement at the thought of being reunited with Bryce. I'd missed him so much. But now, more than ever, I needed to be strong, to protect him from me.

As I approached the tiny Bar Harbor airport, my stomach tied itself into a knot. There were police officers lined up outside; the entrance was barricaded. I rolled down my window and nodded at an officer. "Is everything okay?"

"Yes, Mrs. Windsor. We're expecting you."

I gaped up at him. The police officer knew my name?

"The airport's closed for a private flight. Mr. Windsor's waiting for you—just pull on through." He patted the SUV.

A private flight? Had Bryce just flown in? My thoughts buzzed as I drove through the blockade. The police officers were doing their jobs, all right—there wasn't a sign of the paparazzi anywhere, one slight relief. The press had been chasing us since Gene Windsor was accused of insider trading.

But as I pulled up into the dirt parking lot, any and all relief evaporated. My nerves completely overtook me. There were two black SUVs—which I recognized as belonging to the Windsors—and one random sedan in the parking lot. Bryce's men were stationed outside at various intervals, but Bryce himself was nowhere to be seen.

My phone buzzed. *On the tarmac.*

I glanced over: a small plane was waiting on the grassy runway. Bryce stood outside it, sunglasses on, arms crossed against his broad, muscled chest. I almost started salivating; that was the effect he always had on me. *Damn.*

'Damn' was right because I couldn't touch him. Bryce was like water, water, all around—but no matter how thirsty I was, there would be no drops to drink.

Still, I hustled to the tarmac. I couldn't help but notice how his shirt strained against this powerful chest and arms, his bulging forearms, and how his thick, tousled hair blew back from his forehead. But I'd be lying if I said that it was his good looks that undid me— it was *him*. My husband. My love. The person I wanted to fall asleep with every night, the one I wanted to wake up next to.

The man I had to stay away from.

I reached him but kept my distance. His shoulders sagged.

"Hey," I mumbled.

"Get in." Bryce's voice betrayed no emotion.

"Get in...?"

"The plane." He motioned to the door.

"I can't. I have to go back and get Noah—"

"Noah's with Dale. It's all been taken care of. My father won't know a thing. He's being arrested this afternoon, Chloe. He can't hurt you."

I felt like he'd punched me in the gut. "I don't know what you're talking about—"

Bryce grabbed me by the hips, picked me up like a doll, and stuffed me inside the entrance.

"Hey!" I wrenched free of him.

"Sit down. Get buckled."

"Stop it! You can't make me do this!" I tried maneuvering past him, but his hulking frame blocked the exit.

"The hell I can't. Remember what I said, that I

wouldn't drag you away like a prisoner?" Bryce pulled off his sunglasses so I could see his eyes, revealing the dark circles beneath them. "I lied."

I looked around wildly—there was a pilot seated at the front of the plane and two of Bryce's besuited men in the rear. Not one of them looked at me.

"Noah's safe." Bryce's voice was firm. "I won't let anything happen to him, you know that. Now get in and put your seatbelt on. We're taking off."

"Just where do you think you're taking me?" I hollered.

Bryce motioned for one of his men, who came forward with a roll of duct tape.

"What the hell's that for?" My eyes bulged as the guard measured off a piece—just big enough to fit over my mouth—and ripped it from the roll.

"No more talking, or you'll be wearing that for the rest of the flight." Bryce sat down and fastened his seatbelt.

I opened my mouth, but when the guard moved closer, I shut it.

"Good." My husband sounded exhausted. He leaned back against his seat and closed his eyes. "Let's go. I want to be long gone by the time the feds are on the island."

"Yes, Sir." The pilot closed the door and started clicking various switches in the cockpit.

I glared at Bryce, but it didn't matter: he didn't bother to open his eyes. I side-eyed the guards, but they wouldn't look in my direction. The pilot ignored me, starting the engine and checking his various beeping thingies.

"Unfuckingbelievable," I seethed.

"Chloe." Bryce's voice was a warning.

The guard stood up again, duct tape at the ready.

Unfuckingbelievable. I said it inside my head this time.

And then I glared at my husband—my captor—as he promptly fell asleep in his chair.

The flight was brief, only a few hours. But it was plenty long enough for me to get good and riled up. *How dare he?* Not only had I left my brother behind, but I'd broken my promise to Gene Windsor. Now I was screwed!

I played Bryce's words repeatedly in my head: *"My father won't know a thing. He's being arrested this afternoon, Chloe. He can't hurt you."* Did my husband know Gene had threatened me? If so, how? And if Gene was being arrested, what did that mean for me?

Bryce slept the whole flight, which was for the best. If he was awake, I'd start yelling at him again, and then it would be duct-tape city. *How dare he!*

I sat, glowering, as we began our descent. Once we broke beneath the clouds and saw the sparkling turquoise water, I knew where we were going: Exuma. Bryce had brought me back to the Bahamas, where we'd spent our' honeymoon.' But it wasn't really a honeymoon because we weren't really a couple. We'd been married in name only.

Until that trip. I shivered as the memories washed over me. It was on the remote, gorgeous island that my husband had finally taken me—body, mind, and heart.

I stared out the window. When I turned, I found Bryce awake, watching me. I raised my hand, and he arched an eyebrow. "Yes, Chloe?"

I swallowed hard. "Why did you bring me here?"

"Because you and I have a few things to work out. We can talk about it at the house." He closed his eyes again. I went back to fuming.

We landed, and Bryce motioned for me to go first. He didn't say a word. He slid his sunglasses back on, effectively shutting me out.

How. Dare. He! I was his prisoner, and he wouldn't even look at me. WTF? As usual, it was Bryce's way or the highway.

I'd take the highway, but it wasn't an option as we were on a remote island in the Caribbean. *Grr.*

As soon as we got off the plane, I called Dale. "Is Noah okay? Where are you? I'm so sorry, Bryce made me leave—"

"Chloe, hey, of course, he's okay," Dale interrupted, soothing me. "We're still off-island. I won't bring him back to the house until Gene's gone and the press follows him. You don't have to worry. I'll keep him safe."

"You knew about this, didn't you?" I seethed. "You knew he was taking me somewhere?"

"What's that? You're breaking up. Sorry, let's talk later!" Dale hung up, how convenient.

Bryce didn't say a word to me as we went through customs. All the locals were warm and friendly, greeting us with smiles and wishes for a happy visit. As if!

His driver waited with the Range Rover, a warm smile on the man's face. "Mr. and Mrs. Windsor, we are honored you're joining us again. Sit back and relax—vacation begins now."

"Over my dead body," I hiss-whispered.

Bryce snorted, then stared out the window. He didn't touch me.

I didn't know what to think.

We drove in silence through the island's small downtown, then pulled up to the Windsor's private gate. The driver punched in a code. "The staff prepared some special treats for you." He winked at Bryce in the rearview mirror. "Perfect for a second honeymoon."

I scowled. Bryce remained expressionless, his sunglasses impenetrable.

The Rover maneuvered down the long private drive. Finally, we reached the enormous stucco house, the turquoise ocean winking directly behind it. I remembered every inch of the home—the inside was gorgeous. It opened into an outdoor living space with a stunning infinity pool that overlooked the white-sand beach. John, the driver, carried our bags inside. At least, I hoped one of the bags was mine. I had nothing but the clothes on my back.

The security team followed him inside, and Bryce turned to me. "We should go for a walk while they make sure everything's okay."

I frowned at him. "Do I have a choice about that?"

Bryce glanced back at the driveway, which was about a mile long. "There really isn't any way out of here."

I put my hands on my hips. "Kind of like the plane."

"Kind of." He didn't sound sorry as he headed down toward the beach. I begrudgingly followed, and we stopped to remove our shoes. Once the cool sand was between my toes, I started to feel a little bit better. I ignored Bryce and went down to the water, moaning in pleasure as the warm, pleasant surf washed over my feet.

Bryce rolled up his dress pants and did the same, keeping some distance between us. "That feels good."

I grunted in answer.

Next thing I knew, he'd stripped out of his sunglasses, dress shirt, and pants and did a perfect—of course, it was perfect—dive into the water. When he came up, he wiped his face. He looked better, refreshed. "I know it's a cliche to say it, but come on in. The water's fine."

When I ignored him, he ignored me back. He dove under again. When he resurfaced, he looked like a new man, like the water was some sort of baptism that had cleansed him, making him new again.

I muttered to myself as I took off my tee and my shorts. Thank goodness my husband was a billionaire and had bought me a slew of lingerie, all of it matching. Today I wore a lavender bra and a lacy matching thong —Bryce loved me in a thong.

I dove under, making sure he could take a good look at my ass. Because that's all he was going to be doing—*looking*. I'd made a promise to Gene Windsor and, more importantly, to myself: I was done with Bryce for good. I had Noah to think about. Not only that, I loved Bryce enough to stay true to my word. I owed him that much.

But he'd kidnapped me, and he'd threatened to duct-tape my mouth. I loved him enough to protect him, but I was still pissed.

I dove under again, ass high in the air. *Take a long look.*

That was as close as he was getting.

business

BRYCE

IF CHLOE THOUGHT that she was going to show me her ass and I was just going to let it go, she was dead wrong.

My wife had been wrong about a *lot* of things lately.

Leaving me was the wrong choice. The night she'd packed her bags, after acting so crazy at the wedding, was probably the worst night of my life. I'd sat in my bed, alone, feeling like the biggest fucking idiot that ever lived.

I'd sworn to myself, once things in my previous relationship had fallen apart, that I would never let it happen to me again. That I would never get hurt. So I'd hired a bride, thinking it would keep me safe. And look how that had turned out. I'd fallen in love with Chloe, and she'd left me—her parting words a slap in my face. *You said I made you vulnerable, exposed. You said having me in your life made you lose control.*

It was true. I had said those things, and she'd made me pay the ultimate price for it—losing her.

I hadn't slept since she'd left. Things were so crazy with the company that I just dove into work, trying to manage my father's mess and keep the board on an even keel. The pressure was insane, but I didn't even feel anything. I was like a zombie—without Chloe, it was like I didn't have a heart. I was just a fucking shell of a person going through the motions.

I knew she was in Ellsworth the whole time—she hadn't turned off the location services feature on her phone. I'd had my men outside that rat trap of a motel, watching her day and night. I didn't tell my lawyer that, of course. Just like I didn't tell him I was planning on grabbing her ass, stuffing her onto my private jet, and dragging her to my property on Exuma.

Attorney-client privilege was great and all, but some things were better left unsaid. Like the fact that I was kidnapping my wife.

Now said wife's ass was right next to me, in a thong no less, and she wouldn't come near me. I couldn't figure her out. When we'd first met, she'd been so nervous. I, of course, had been a dick. But once I'd let my guard down and opened up to her, I saw the truth about Chloe. She was a good person. She actually had a kind heart. She'd been through hell with her mother dying and with her deadbeat father and his sleaze of a wife, but she hadn't given up on life. She'd married a stranger for money just so she could protect her brother.

I'd fallen hard for her. I thought she loved me, too.

There weren't many people in my world like Chloe. I'd never met anyone—except for my own mother—who loved that much, who would put themselves in a difficult situation to take care of someone else. I'd never met a person as selfless as Chloe. My relationship experience had consisted of the Felicia-Joneses of the world: people who were self-obsessed, lacked self-awareness, and didn't acknowledge or seem to care how their actions impacted others. "Something wasn't right." That was Felicia's explanation for cheating on me and calling off our wedding.

Thanks, Felicia! I'd dodged a bullet with that one.

My ex was an ass, but *I* was the real asshole: she was who she was, but I'd been the one to date her. And then I let what happened between us make me so paranoid, I had trouble opening up when something real came along. *Ugh.*

I certainly hadn't planned on falling for my hired

bride. But the truth was, once Chloe and I connected, I knew it was meant to be. It was easy with her. She was my best friend, the one person I could be myself with.

And then she'd gone crazy at the wedding, wearing that revealing red dress, getting drunk, and going after Felicia. Chloe hadn't been herself that night. Why had she done that and then left? I knew there was more to the story, but she wasn't talking.

Fine. I would get it out of her one way or the other. The most important thing was that she was back and that she was *mine*. She might think she had a choice about that, but I was going to show her otherwise.

We were meant to be together. She didn't crash into my life by mistake. I didn't hire a stranger and fall in love with her by accident.

Like I said, it was meant to be.

This was the most crucial moment of my career. I was the acting CEO of Windsor Enterprises, the only job I'd ever wanted since I was a kid. I had big plans for the company, for the direction I wanted to take it in now that my father had finally been forced into stepping down. But I couldn't do anything until things in my marriage were settled.

What I'd said to Chloe had been true: she made me vulnerable, and I didn't do vulnerable. But we'd crossed a line. There was no going back.

She dove underwater again, her smooth, perfectly round ass in the air. She was crazy if she thought she was going to make it through the weekend without me taking her.

She was mine, and I always took what was mine.

change of heart

CHLOE

"Mr. and Mrs. Windsor." The security guard stood at the water's edge, fluffy robes and towels in each hand. He kept his gaze averted, firmly fixed on the horizon. "The property's cleared. I've been alerted there's about to be a press conference."

"Thank you." Bryce climbed out, unabashed, as rivulets of water coursed down his muscular frame and over his tight boxer briefs. He took the items and then nodded. "You're dismissed."

Bryce waited until the other man was back inside the house, then held out a robe for me. "Put this on. We need to go watch the news."

"Is this about your father?" I still hadn't spoken a word to him, but it seemed cruel not to ask.

"Yes—I don't want to miss it."

I quickly joined him on the beach and toweled myself dry, grateful for the robe's coverage.

Bryce's gaze flicked down my body. "I had Midge pack a suitcase for you. Go get changed and meet me in the living room. I wouldn't want you to sit around in that wet thong."

Ah, so he *had* been looking. I raised my chin, struggling to appear nonchalant. "Fine."

"Fine." He motioned toward the house.

Damn him! He sounded much calmer than I felt. I tightened the robe around me and hustled to the bedroom, grateful to be away from him for a moment. I was a mess. Angry that he'd separated me from my brother, pissed that he'd threatened to have my mouth taped shut, afraid of what his father would do—all of that was mixed with a deep, undeniable longing.

I craved him. Being around my husband made me realize how much I'd missed him. Having Bryce close but not touching him was torture. In the midst of my anger, memories of how good we'd been together kept breaking through to the surface. Being pissed at him was a blessing. It kept the other feelings underwater, where they belonged.

Inside our room, I refused to look at the bed. That was where he'd taken me for the first time. I remembered that night so clearly; it was painful. I'd pledged to be his and only his, and he'd rewarded me by hand-cuffing me and penetrating me, making me lose my goddamned mind. I'd come so hard I'd seen stars. And he'd been so tender with me afterward, cradling me to his chest, telling me I was his forever. *Don't, Chloe. Don't think about it.*

I numbly moved to the bureau; I needed to get dressed. The staff had already unpacked our suitcases. I found a ton of sexy underwear, all with matching bras, in one of the drawers. There was a folded note on top of them.

I don't know why you left, but I sure miss you. Wear a thong while you're down there, okay?

Give a girl some hope!

~ Midge

Tears pricked my eyes as I folded the note. Midge, my maid, had always been good to me. She'd probably been upset that I left without saying goodbye. I hadn't known her for long, but she'd become like family.

I obediently put another thong on and then scoured the drawers for something comfortable. Everything Midge had packed was insanely expensive and formfitting. Not that I was surprised by that! I pulled on a cropped T-shirt and a pair of soft black leggings that probably cost more than a week's stay at the Ellsworth motel. I checked my reflection in the mirror. The outfit, though casual, did everything to show off my curves. *God bless you, Midge.* Even though I'd vowed to keep my distance from Bryce, I still wanted to look good.

The bathroom had a brand-new toothbrush and an array of designer cosmetics. I quickly brushed my teeth and hair, swiped on some mascara and lip gloss, and went out to the living room. No matter what had happened between us, no matter that we could never be together again, I wanted to be beside Bryce to watch the news of his father's arrest.

He was sitting on the couch in front of an enormous flatscreen television, bourbon in hand. The breeze from the beach blew in, making the room comfortable and cool. Bryce's feet were up on the table in front of him; he'd changed into sweat shorts and a T-shirt, all the better to show off his muscled physique. But despite the bourbon and the lack of a suit, he looked stressed. A line furrowed in between his brows as he stared at the screen.

I sank down next to him as the news anchor addressed the camera. "Earlier this afternoon, billionaire Gene Windsor was taken into custody." An image of Bryce's father, in handcuffs, being led from his gorgeous Maine estate filled the screen. Gene looked dapper and somewhat defiant in his linen trousers and white dress shirt, what was left of his thinning hair flapping in the ocean breeze. The federal agents led him to the dock and put him onto a boat.

"The founder and CEO of Windsor Enterprises is accused of insider trading involving a real-estate index fund that netted him close to a billion dollars," the reporter continued. "If found guilty, the mogul could be fined up to twenty-five million dollars and receive a twenty-year jail sentence."

The image cut to a family picture of Gene, his late wife, Bryce, and his brothers Colby and Jake. "In his absence, Windsor Enterprises will be run by his three sons—Bryce, Colby, and Jake Windsor. His eldest son Bryce was named acting CEO this morning." A video of Bryce walking, flanked by Regina Hernandez and some other board members, filled the screen.

"Despite a recent scandal involving his wife, Bryce Windsor is highly regarded and seen as a competent predecessor to his father." There were pictures of Bryce and me eating dinner at the restaurant on Spruce Island. Blessedly, they didn't show any of me fighting Felicia Jones. "Still, Windsor Enterprises's stock declined four-percent today. Investors report they are cautiously optimistic about the change in leadership but are waiting to see how the younger Windsor transitions. A spokesperson for the family, Olivia Jensen, said that Bryce Windsor had taken the weekend to spend with his family before beginning work next week."

Bryce turned off the television, and we sat in silence for a few minutes. "Well, I guess it's official." He drained his glass.

"Are you okay?"

He shrugged his big shoulders. "We knew it was coming."

"What happens next? Is the trial going to start soon?"

"I talked to his lawyers this morning—they expect it to start in a month," Bryce answered. "They said he's going to have to stay in prison, no bail because he's a flight risk."

"So he has to stay for a whole month before the trial even *starts*?" I had no idea how any of this worked.

He nodded.

"I can't picture your father in prison." Gene Windsor

had more money than God. I'd never seen him without his Gucci loafers on. He insisted his staff wear old-school tuxedos and maid's uniforms.

"You know how nasty my old man is—he'll be all right in prison. Not sure how he's going to adjust to a twin bed and the dining hall at first, but then again, he *did* commit a federal crime. So it's a little late to feel sorry for him."

"Do you?" I was genuinely curious. "Feel sorry for him?"

Bryce shrugged again.

"Listen... I'm sorry about what they said—about the 'recent scandal.' I'm *so* sorry." I cringed like I did every time I saw or heard something about it on the news.

"Chloe." He turned to me. "You've already apologized. I just want to know why you did it."

I nervously twisted my fingers together. "I don't know how to answer that."

"Is that because you don't want to answer? Or because you can't?" His gaze was steady, searching.

"You've already heard what I have to say. I got drunk because I was feeling insecure, and then I got into a fight. It's really not anything deeper than that. It's as immature as it sounds," I said miserably.

Gene Windsor had known precisely what he was doing. The internet was forever, and so was my shame. *Chloe Shows Her True Colors.* You could take the girl out of grimy East Boston, but perhaps you couldn't take the griminess out of the girl. I'd never live down that fight with Felicia; by proxy, neither would Bryce.

"It's not that big of a deal." Bryce shrugged.

I blinked at him. "You're kidding, right? They just mentioned it on national news!"

"I'm not kidding." He got up and poured another drink, then resumed his spot on the couch. "It's not a big enough deal for you to walk out on me in the middle of the night and drag Noah with you. I want to know the truth. I want to know why you left."

I longed to tell him, but his father's words came back to me again. *"You have a lot to lose. When I say that, I'm not just thinking of your marriage. I'm thinking of your brother."*

Bryce's phone buzzed. He cursed as he glanced at it. "I have to take this. It's the board."

As he stalked outside, I headed into the kitchen for a glass of water. My phone buzzed, too, and I considered throwing it in the ocean. What would it be like, I mused, to be free from the outside world? No one could threaten me, track me, and if they wrote headlines about me? I would never see them—it would be bliss. But I had my brother to think about, so I opened my messages.

There were more than I cared to count. Three from Akira, two from Olivia Jensen, and a couple from Dale. There was also one from a number I didn't recognize.

I checked Dale's first. *Back on the island, all is well,* he wrote.

The second text was a picture of Noah with Boss, his puppy. *Together again.*

Thank you, Dale, I texted back. *Even though you set me up.*

He didn't respond, but the message became marked as "read," so at least I knew he'd gotten it. I stared at the picture of Noah and Boss. My brother would be thrilled to be back on the island with the puppy, able to sleep in his own room and enjoy being spoiled by the staff. Chef would probably bake him cookies and make all of his favorite meals. Noah would officially never speak to me again when I came back from the Bahamas and made him leave.

Sighing, I opened the messages from Akira.

Jim Wright said you went to Exuma with Bryce, she wrote.

WTH?

I thought you were breaking the contract.

I didn't answer her. If I told her that Bryce had stuffed me onto his private plane, threatened to tape my mouth shut, then dragged me to his private, guarded estate, she'd call the local police. The last thing Bryce needed right now was more bad press.

Olivia Jensen's messages were next. The curvy, fiery redhead was Gene Windsor's public relations person, and she was not my favorite. *Please send pics from this weekend,* she wrote. *We need them for Bryce's launch week. And I need to meet with you one-on-one when you guys get back.*

Ugh, Olivia was apparently still working furiously to control the public image of the Windsor family. I hadn't spoken with her since my meltdown at the wedding. She was probably very unhappy with me.

Will do, I texted back. Great, now Bryce and I needed to take selfies!

I opened the last text from the unknown number. It was probably junk, but I was a big believer in cleaning out my notifications. *Dear Mrs. Windsor,* it read. *This firm represents Gene Windsor. Attached is a secure link to a private message.*

My stomach sank. Gene Windsor had been arrested, but apparently, it didn't matter: he would never leave me the hell alone. I looked outside. Bryce was stalking the pool deck, phone glued to his ear. I took a deep, shuddery breath and clicked the link.

Gene Windsor appeared on the screen, wearing the same white dress shirt he'd been arrested in. It was a video; he was smiling his usual smug smile. "Chloe, how nice of you to open this. I trust by now, the news of my arrest has been broadcast. I understand my son planned on bringing you to Exuma—he's never been one to listen to common sense. If this message was sent, it means you're directly violating our agreement."

I gripped the edge of the counter. *Oh my God, oh my god—*

"Lucky for you," Gene continued, "because of my impending incarceration, I've had a...change of heart, I suppose you'd call it. I can't ignore the timing of all this. I didn't know I'd be arrested and incarcerated as soon as today. But because that's the case, I need something from you."

I held my breath.

"These are your new instructions, and they are non-negotiable. I need you to go back home with Bryce. Stay there with him and pretend to be the perfect, loving wife. No more drunken scandals, no more fighting. But from this moment forward, you need to understand something: you work for me now."

He smiled at the camera, and an icy chill needled my back.

"You will do what I say when I say it. If you want to keep your brother away from your drunken, low-life parents—and don't bother asking them to back off, they're already on my payroll—you will follow my instructions to the letter. My firm will send you messages. Say nothing to Bryce, or you will be *very* sorry. Good day."

The screen went blank, and so did my mind. I stared at the phone.

You work for me now.

If you want to keep your brother...you will do what I say.

I couldn't believe that Gene had changed his mind so abruptly. Part of me was relieved that he'd instructed me to stay with Bryce, but I knew better than to trust that feeling. Gene Windsor was bad news. He hated me, and my brother was nothing more than a pawn to him, a way to control me.

I'd been in trouble before, but this was different. Noah and I had been away from the island, away from the family. If I'd thrown my stupid cell phone out, maybe they never would've been able to find me. Even if they'd brought a lawsuit, we could've hidden. We could be safe right now.

But we weren't. We were a long way from safe.

Gene Windsor might be in jail, but he was sending me back into his territory—enemy territory.

And now the enemy was my master.

primary

CHLOE

"Who was that?" Bryce was suddenly behind me.

"It was nothing—I was just watching a news clip." I forced myself to sound casual as I turned off my phone.

His gaze flicked over me. "I'm going to sit by the pool for a while. Come with me." It was a command, not a question. But I'd one-hundred-bajillion times rather follow Bryce's orders than his father's.

It didn't seem I had much of a choice about that.

I couldn't process what the old man had said to me—that he'd put my father and Lydia on his payroll, that he'd take Noah away from me, that if I said anything to Bryce, I would be *very sorry*. I stared at my husband's back as I followed him outside. I yearned to tell him about the position I was in, but I was too afraid. Gene Windsor was scary as shit.

At least I was with Bryce. At least I could stay with him...for now.

He sank down onto one of the couches facing the pool and the ocean. I sat beside him, close but not too close.

He stared out at the water. "I brought you down here so that we could be alone. I thought I could talk some sense into you."

"Okay..."

"But you seem a million miles away, Chloe. You're not yourself. And you haven't been."

I blew out a deep breath. Now that I knew I could go back to him—now that I knew it was safe for Noah—I could let my guard down, at least a little.

"It's true, haven't been myself," I admitted. "I'm embarrassed about what happened and stressed about you taking over for your father. I want to be there for you, but I feel like I messed up too bad."

He glanced at me. "You want to be there for me?"

My shoulders sagged. "Of course I do."

"Well... That's a start."

We sat silently for a moment, but at least it wasn't as awful.

"I guess I shouldn't have threatened to tape your

mouth shut." Bryce still didn't sound sorry. "And I shouldn't have forced you onto the plane like that."

"No, you shouldn't have," I agreed.

The silence stretched out between us again. He was right next to me, but it felt like we were a million miles apart. Was it only a week ago that he'd held me in his arms, and I'd felt like he was my whole world? I didn't know how to find my way back to him, to us.

He waited, and when I didn't say anything further, he sighed. "This is awkward as fuck. There's only one thing to do."

"What's that?"

"Get your ass in the bedroom, Chloe."

"*What?*"

"Or we can take care of business right here." He shrugged. "The guards won't look in our direction—I'll make damn sure of that."

I started to object, but he reached over and clamped an enormous hand over my mouth. "I'm not actually sorry about the tape—I wish I had some right now. Let's go, Mrs. Windsor. There's only one way to get things back to normal."

With that, he hoisted me up. Wrapping his free arm around me and pressing me against him, he dragged me down the hall. Bryce had an erection brewing, and he blatantly pressed it against me. I fought him, and he laughed, a dark sound. He got harder as I struggled, throbbing against me.

"Fight me, Chloe—that's it. That'll make this even hotter."

He pressed his cock against me, and I yelled obscenities into the palm of his hand. How dare he?

"Keep it up, babe." He thrust his hips, erection grinding against me.

Fuck. With his hand clamped over my mouth, his other bulging forearm gripping my midsection, and his dick pressed against my ass—I was getting wet. Undeniably, inconveniently wet. I wouldn't be able to hide it from him once he took my clothes off...

Please God, let him get inside me quick. I would never admit it, but Bryce was right: I needed him inside me. I yearned for him to claim me, to make me his, to take me back—to make me his wife again. It had only been a few days, but it felt like forever.

And I'd been keeping secrets from him, which made me feel separate. It made me feel alone when all I wanted to do was be one with him.

Gene's slimy message was on the periphery of my thoughts—but God bless Bryce, he made me forget. He shoved me onto the bed and removed his hand from my mouth. Then he put his full, luscious lips to mine, and the rest of the world fell away. His tongue darted inside, seeking mine. They connected, lashing each other, and I moaned.

"That's right." He sounded so smug, but I didn't care; I was too busy ripping off his clothes. I pulled the T-shirt over his head and sighed in relief as I ran my hands down his lightly tanned, smooth skin. I'd been craving this, craving him. His muscles rippled beneath my fingers. Touching his bare skin felt like coming home.

He was on top of me on the bed, all over me—his hands in my hair, taking off my tank, somehow getting the leggings off, the head of his cock already brushing against my wet slit.

"You're already so wet for me." Bryce radiated smug energy as he notched his cock inside me, then withdrew.

"So?" I asked archly. "What're you going to do about it?" I spread my legs and grabbed his ass, positioning him at my entrance.

Bryce laughed, a low, rumbling sound that I felt inside me.

"Don't laugh at me," I said hoarsely. "I need you."

"Now you need me." He inched inside and then pulled out again, torturing me. "You didn't seem to want me very much the other night when you ran out."

"Bryce, please..." I writhed beneath him. "I'm sorry. I

was embarrassed. I didn't know what to do." I grabbed his ass again, possessively pulling him back.

"Leaving wasn't the right answer." The joking tone dropped from his voice.

"I said I was sorry," I panted. "Please, Bryce—I'll do anything."

He pulsed his cock inside me, then withdrew. "Don't ever leave me again."

"I won't. I promise." My eyes pricked with tears. I had no idea if I had any right to promise that.

"I've been out of my goddamned mind the past couple of days." He entered me again, deeper, and then pulled out.

"I'm sorry." I thrashed beneath him. I would say anything, promise anything—and of course, I wanted it to be true. "Just *please*, take me, I've missed you so much—"

He clamped his mouth over mine and thrust his tip inside me, once, twice, three times. *Fuck!* I was so wet for him, so ready. I squeezed his ass cheeks, and he knew exactly what to do.

He entered me all the way, and we both cried out.

Bryce thrust over and over again. Driving, deep, unforgiving. I grabbed his hips, his ass, scratched his back, anything to keep him close to me, to feel his power as he claimed me. I was impatient, wanting to feel all of him, desperate for him to overtake me. Bryce's body listened to mine, his urgent, deep strokes taking me to the edge almost immediately.

He leaned up, all glorious muscle, a Greek God of a man. I greedily drank in the sight of him—my husband, my love, my everything.

He put his palm on top of my sex and continued to fuck me hard.

"Come in me," I begged. I was on the edge, and I wanted him there with me.

His strokes got deeper, even more urgent. "Chloe!" He filled me as my body clenched around him, and I shattered, seeing stars. Nothing compared to this, to the feeling of us coming together, being one, his body part of mine, part of me. I clung to him as our orgasms subsided, and we held each other, hearts pounding, as we came back to earth.

I brought my mouth against his ear. "I love you." What was the point of lying anymore?

"I love you, too." Bryce collapsed beside me and pulled me onto his massive chest.

We fell asleep like that and, for a precious few hours, I forgot about everything...except him.

SEVEN

a girl like me

CHLOE

IT WAS A WEEKEND OF PRETENDING. There were no further messages from Gene Windsor. Akira gave up texting and left me alone. There wasn't a word from Elena or from Olivia Jensen. Everyone knew where I was and what I was doing.

They knew it was useless to do anything but wait.

I pretended that everything was fine. Bryce and I didn't talk more about why I'd run away in the middle of the night. I didn't tell him about his father's threats —in fact, I pushed them out of my mind.

All I was thinking about, my only focus, was my husband.

He'd been right, of course—as soon as we'd made

love, everything became easier between us. It was as if some magic spell had been broken. I didn't leave his side. In turn, he didn't take his hands off me. We didn't talk much, but the silence had transformed into something peaceful and companionable. We fell asleep each night wrapped in each other's arms. In the mornings, Bryce cradled me against his chest.

I refused to think about the bad things.

I knew that Gene wouldn't let me have this—not for long. But I had my husband for now, and I didn't want to waste a moment of it.

I also ignored that our weekend was coming to an end. I'd been so angry about being forced to go, but all resistance had melted away. I wanted nothing more than to stay in our happy bubble, separated from the rest of the world.

The morning of our return flight, we sat out on the pool deck under an umbrella. "Huh." Bryce peered at his phone. "I'm surprised to see this."

"What?" He handed it to me—there was a picture of his brother, Colby, walking the beach with an attractive blond woman. "I thought Olivia Jensen told your brothers no dating right now." She'd also told them they both had to get married sooner rather than later. Neither Jake nor Colby was happy about any of it!

Bryce took the phone back and frowned at it. "She

did. I don't know who the blond is. I'll talk to him about it tonight."

My stomach dropped. As much as I wanted to go back and see my brother, I was in no rush to return to reality. "How do you feel about going to work tomorrow?"

As he sat back in his lounger, Bryce reached for my hand. "I feel better about everything now. It'll be fine."

I squeezed his fingers, but then I had that Sunday-night 'I forgot to do my homework" feeling. "Crap! Olivia Jensen asked me to take pictures of us and send them to her."

"She's a pain in the ass, but come here." Bryce pulled me onto his lap and held up his phone. "Let's just get it over with. She's easier to deal with head-on."

We smiled for our pictures and then held hands down to the beach. We snapped more selfies with the turquoise water in the background. Bryce wrapped his arm around me, pulling me against his big chest, and I couldn't help but smile. "This has been a great weekend," I admitted.

Bryce kissed the top of my head. "Next time, I won't kidnap you."

"Ha." *But what if Gene makes me leave once and for all?*

I shoved the thought away and clung to my husband.

"Listen." He nuzzled his face against my neck, his scruffy beard tickling my bare skin. "Things are going to be busy for me when we get back. That's part of the reason why I wanted this weekend with you. I need to know that we're okay—that *you're* okay."

"I'm okay." *Right now, here with you, all is well in my world.*

"What about when we go back? Are you going to have a hard time at the house?"

"I don't think so..." I hesitated for a moment. "What's it going to be like? Are the paparazzi going to be everywhere still?"

"I don't think the coverage will be as intense. There's going to be a lot of focus on the investigation, and more about the upcoming trial."

I nodded. "But Olivia's working for your father. So there's still a script to follow." I was concerned about what, exactly, my role would be in all this. Previously, Olivia had orchestrated dramatic run-ins with Bryce's ex in order to generate interest from the press. I couldn't deal with any more Felicia-Jones drama!

"I'm sure there will be. But we're not getting involved in any more drama—I already told our team that. I'm going to work, and you're staying home. I'll be working remotely most of the time, but I might have to do some traveling. Will you come with me?"

"Of course." My heart lifted a little. As long as I didn't let myself think about Gene's threats, the idea of being back with Bryce was wonderful. "I'd like that."

"So... Are we okay?" He wrapped his arms around me and pulled me close. "You seem more like yourself now that we've been... You know." He playfully arched an eyebrow.

"Ha." I buried my face against his chest, inhaling his spicy, masculine scent mixed with the balmy ocean air. "I do feel better."

"Me too." Bryce tightened his embrace. "But I have to ask, are you staying? I can't handle you running out on me again, Chloe. There's too much at stake, and I'm not just talking about business."

"Yes. I'm staying, Bryce. You have my word." I'd been selfish, letting myself pretend all weekend. Why stop now?

"I'm glad to hear it, Mrs. Windsor." He pressed his cheek against mine.

I held onto the man I loved for dear life, wishing the moment would never end. But deep down, I knew that the comfort and happiness I felt had an expiration date.

There was no such thing as a happy ending for a girl like me.

The good news? The security guard who'd threatened to tape my mouth shut was *not* on our flight back to Bar Harbor.

The bad news? Once we arrived home, I was officially in Gene Windsor's territory. And that was not a safe place to be.

Still, Maine looked different when we arrived. The colors were brighter than when I'd left three days ago, the mountains more majestic, the water more clear and pristine. I coined it "The Bryce Effect." Everything looked better now that I was back in my husband's arms.

Once we disembarked the plane, my internet service was unfortunately strong. I had a ton of emails, calls, and texts download as soon as we were on the road back to Northeast Harbor. There was a message from Elena (*I'm so glad you came to your senses!*) and another from Olivia Jensen (*More bikini pics, pls*). Akira had left me a weary-sounding voicemail, instructing me to call her once I was back in the States. I decided to wait until I settled in—it would be easier to tell her once it was official.

Bryce was on the phone with board members during both the car and boat ride from the Bar Harbor airport, but I didn't mind. I snuggled against him, happy that we were going home, grateful that I'd be reunited with my brother soon, relieved that Gene Windsor seemed to have forgotten about me for a couple of days.

Still, I was nervous about returning to Somes Island, the private island where Bryce and his father each had homes. When I'd left, I'd woken up half the staff in the middle of the night in my attempt to escape. And I'd turned to Bryce's maid, Hazel—of all people—to help me. I had no idea how I'd be received or if the staff would treat me like a pariah.

But Captain Johnny gave us a friendly smile as we boarded the *Jules*, Bryce's pristine boat. The older gentleman didn't say another word, bless his heart. I was thrilled Bryce hadn't fired him—he'd been the one to whisk me and Noah off-island in the middle of the night after (lots) of begging.

Much to my surprise, the staff was waiting for us once we landed and climbed up to the house from the private dock. "Mr. Windsor, Mrs. Windsor." Several of the maids, dressed in their immaculate uniforms, bowed at us. Midge took it one step further and hustled over, knocking me off balance with a huge hug. "I'm so glad you're here," she whispered in my ear.

Hazel was waiting, too. "Mrs. Windsor." She bowed her head. Bryce's most loyal, and longest-term, employee was dressed as usual in her stiffly ironed maid's uniform, her spindly legs encased in black stockings. Her thin, dyed-black hair was pulled up into a bun, and her lined lips were puckered.

She raised her head, her cool inspecting me. "We're happy to have you back."

I blinked at her, surprised and embarrassed. "H-Hi Hazel. Thank you."

Chef kissed his fingers and declared that we would have a feast that evening in my honor. "Nada sofisticado," he said. "That means 'nothing too fancy.' I know how you are."

The kind welcome, which I felt I didn't deserve, warmed my heart. "Thank you. It's nice to be home."

"Noah's around the corner with Boss." Midge nodded toward the side of the house. "Dale bought him a drone. They're trying to train the puppy to fetch from it."

"Oh jeez," I groaned.

Bryce, still on the phone, quickly kissed my cheek. "Go see your brother. I'll meet you inside," he mouthed.

"Okay." I smiled at him, and it was a dangerously genuine smile. How could it not be? We were home on his tiny, gorgeous island in Maine, the sun was shining, and his staff had welcomed me back with open arms. Since my mother died, I hadn't felt at peace anywhere. But now Bryce's mega-mansion was familiar and comforting, even though living in such an opulent residence was still foreign to me. It was the people that made me feel at home.

I headed around the corner, the ocean wind whipping my ponytail as I inhaled the familiar, heady scent of the brisk Maine ocean. Exuma was beautiful, but nothing quite compared to Maine—the rolling green lawn spread out before me, the dark blue-green waves crashed against the rocky shore, and an eagle soared toward the woods. The surroundings were awe-inspiring. Tears pricked my eyes as I spotted Noah out on the grass with Dale, flying a drone, Boss the puppy jumping up and down excitedly.

How could I have taken Noah away from all of this?

What if I had to do it again?

"Chloe—hey!" A familiar voice called out, interrupting my troubled thoughts. Bryce's youngest brother, Colby, had his arm around an attractive blond woman as they headed up from the beach.

Colby wore a sweatshirt, a pair of golf shorts, and his usual grin. The baby of the family, he was usually in good spirits and often had a twinkle in his eye. Colby was shorter than Bryce but was still six feet tall. He had one lone dimple, blue eyes, and enormous shoulders. With his tousled hair and chiseled good looks, he was every inch a Windsor.

The young woman accompanying him was stunning, with long, thick blond hair, brown eyes, a light tan, and a curvy, athletic build. She wore denim short-shorts and a formfitting tank that showed off her figure. She had that white, rich, All-American look going like she was a head cheerleader, the president of her sorority, and an Instagram influencer all rolled into one.

"I was worried you weren't coming back." He grinned at me.

"Guess I can't stay away." I gave him a quick hug. "How are you?"

"Okay, even though Dad got taken into custody yesterday." He scrubbed a hand over his eyes for a moment.

"I know—I'm so sorry."

"Thank you. That means a lot." He shook it off and smiled again. "Hey, this is my friend, Tate. Tate, this is Chloe, my brother Bryce's wife."

"Nice to see you." She gave me a dazzling smile and a firm handshake.

"Nice to meet you. Do you live up here? Or are you visiting?" I was still surprised that Olivia Jensen had allowed Colby to start seeing someone. She'd been dead-set against the younger Windsor men dating anyone new while the press was still swarming the family.

"I'm from Boston." Her gaze flicked down me, taking in every inch with her cool stare.

"Nice. Me too."

She smiled again, but I noticed that although her teeth were a mesmerizing, bright white, her smile seemed flat—it did nothing to light up her face. "Oh—I know where you're from."

There was an awkward silence.

"Want to go check out the drone?" Colby asked, smoothing over the uncomfortable moment. "I think Dale put a treat for Boss on there—the dog's been chasing the thing all over the island." He laughed.

"Sure," I said.

"Absolutely." Tate straightened her shoulders and stuck her chest out.

Colby released her and headed toward Dale and Noah. "Hey, guys! Can I give that thing a whirl?"

Tate and I followed him. "So..." I wasn't sure how to approach her. "What part of Boston are you from?"

"The South End." She gave me another long look as if she was sizing me up.

"Oh." The South End was where Accommodating was located. But a lot of other things were there, too. Galleries, wine bars, dog parks...

She leaned closer. "I'm so glad you're here. I didn't want to be the only one."

"The only...? The only girl?" I suddenly had a sick feeling in my stomach.

"No, silly. The only *escort*." Tate winked at me, then hustled to Colby's side. She joined him, linking her hand through his. Then she looked over her shoulder at me and smiled.

It was not a nice smile.

reeling

CHLOE

"CHLOE!" Noah hugged me hard, then told me how great it was to be back. The drone was amazing, the dog treats were gourmet, Boss could already follow commands, and Chef had made him about five million frappes over the weekend. I smiled in all the right places, nodding my head where appropriate. I was genuinely happy to be reunited with my brother, but I couldn't focus on his words.

I was reeling. Tate was an *escort*? She'd said she was from the South End of Boston. Did that mean she was from Accommodating? Elena hadn't said anything about sending another girl up here. But how else could

Tate know about me? My mind whirled as we played with the dog, my brother's happy laughter filling the air.

I couldn't wait to get back to Bryce and tell him what had happened. He needed to know if there was another escort here as soon as possible. I didn't understand it. *Why* and *how* was she here? Elena was an intelligent business owner. It didn't seem likely that she'd sabotage my position by sending another girl to work for the Windsor family, doubling our risk of exposure.

The drone landed, and Dale declared it in need of a charge—I took that as my opportunity to escape. I hugged my brother again, ruffling his hair until he squirmed away. Then I headed for the house, anxious to update Bryce.

"Chloe, wait, I'll come with you!" Tate gave me another dazzling, yet didn't-reach-her-eyes, smile.

She made a kissy face at Colby. "I'll see you at the house. Okay, babe?"

"Yeah, babe. Sounds good." He grinned, his lone dimple flashing. Colby seemed positively charmed by her. There was a lot of 'babe' being thrown around for two people who had just started dating.

Tate waited until we were away from the others to speak to me. A scowl crept over her features, a deep crease forming between her perfectly groomed brows. "I need you to keep what I told you a secret. You can't say anything to anybody."

"Um..." Confused, I shook my head. "I'm assuming Colby knows, right? Isn't he the one who hired you?"

"No! He doesn't know I'm an escort. I bumped into him at the pool club and started talking to him. He bought me a drink—the rest is history." She shrugged.

"What?" I stopped walking. "So who hired you?"

"Can't say." Tate shrugged again, and it was maddening. She was my age but seemed younger, a teenager with a bad freaking attitude. "But that's the point—Colby's into me, and I'd like to keep it that way. I need this job. I need the money."

"So who *is* paying you?"

She turned to face me, flipping her hair in the process. As pretty as I'd thought her earlier, her face was transformed by the sneer. "Someone who doesn't like you."

"*What?*"

Tate puffed her admirable chest out. "If you tell anybody about me, you're going to pay. I'll go public with the truth about where you came from. So keep your mouth shut." She was sounding less like a prep-school cheerleader and more like a toughie from my old neighborhood by the second.

"If you didn't want anybody to know, why did you tell me?"

She laughed. "Because my client *wants* you to know. They want you to know that you're being watched and that they know the truth about you."

My stomach sank. "Did Gene Windsor hire you?"

"I wish." Tate snorted. "I'd like some of that money. But my client's rich, too. I'm getting paid a small fortune to blow Colby, keep him happy, and more importantly, torture your lying ass. Everyone thinks you're actually Bryce's wife, right?"

"I *am* actually his wife."

"Ha!" Tate leaned closer, the minty smell of her breath wafting over me. "You know what I mean. Girls like us don't marry guys like these."

I bristled. "I *already* married him."

She snorted again, nostrils flaring. The real Tate was not a pretty sight. "I might be the best thing that's happened to you—you need a reality check. My client might want me to sleep with your husband—to remind you that you're just like me. Replaceable."

"My husband wouldn't be interested," I said stiffly.

"We'll see." She stuck her chest out again.

I shook my head. "What do you want from me?"

"For now, I want you to keep your mouth shut. After that? I'll let you know." With a final hair toss, Tate hiked up her shorts so her ass cheeks were prominently hanging out. She sauntered inside the house as if she owned the place.

I didn't follow her inside. I sank down onto the steps, head swimming. *Fuuuck.* Gene Windsor might be gone from the island, but now I had to deal with Tate the Adolescent Escort. Someone had hired her to get close to Colby—and more importantly, to get close to *me*. Tate was nasty, but she'd seemed honest when she'd said it wasn't Gene that had hired her.

So who could it be? What other enemies did I have?

My step monster Lydia, for sure. But she and my father didn't have the money to pay for a high-end escort.

That left Felicia Jones, Bryce's heinous ex. *She wouldn't!*

But...would she? Did she hate me enough to plant someone on the island just to torture my ass?

With shaking hands, I texted Elena. *There's a new girl here—she says she's an escort from the South End. Does she work for you?*

The madam immediately texted back.

What? That's crazy.

I haven't sent anyone up there. I wouldn't do that.

I stared at my phone, not knowing what to do or what to think.

"Oh my God! I thought you were never coming back!" Daphne hurtled up the stairs toward me. Gene's estranged wife wore a crop top that showed off the barest hint of a baby bump and black yoga pants. Her long dark hair was up in a bun, her makeup minimal and perfect, and she smelled luxurious and rich, like a trust-fund scented shower gel.

"Hey!" I was surprisingly relieved to see her. Daphne had scared the crap out of me when we'd first met, but like a fungus, she'd grown on me. And at the moment, she was a welcome distraction from the sting of Tate's words.

She hugged me, then pulled away, scowling. "I forgot I wasn't speaking to you!" She crossed her toned arms against her chest. "You ran off in the middle of the night and didn't return any of my texts. *Rude*. Where the hell have you been?"

She suspiciously eyed me up and down. "Your skin's glowing. So let me rephrase that—where the hell have you been besides in the Bahamas getting banged by Bryce? I've been dying up here! Gene got arrested, every-thing's a mess, his assets might be frozen if they set bail —ugh! And I'm getting fat!"

"You look great. You're not getting fat; you're *pregnant*. It's about time you looked like you were having a baby. How far along are you now?"

"A couple of months." She grinned. "Stupid Michael Jones still won't speak to me, so I had my lawyers send him an offer."

Daphne was married to Gene Windsor, but she'd had a brief affair with Micheal Jones, Felicia's father. Michael Jones was also married. The whole thing was a mess. Daphne had planned to leave Gene for Michael, but he'd ghosted her and decided to stay with his wife. In the end, Gene had agreed to remain married to Daphne—at least for the moment.

Growing up, I thought rich people didn't have any problems. That their lives were perfect. It turned out they were just as messed up, if not more so, than the rest of us!

"If he waives all parental rights," she continued, "I'll accept ten million dollars in a lump-sum child support payment. Gene thinks I'm lowballing him, but whatever. I just want to be done with it. He's never going to leave his wife, you know? These old bastards say one thing when they want something from you, but it's another story once the wife finds out."

I laughed. "You haven't changed much since we last talked." Daphne's morals were downright questionable, but at least she was honest about who she was. "How are you holding up with Gene being arrested?"

"Not great." She sighed and sat down next to me. "You know what's weird?"

I shook my head.

"I'm worried about him." Daphne wrinkled her nose. "He's been so miserable these last few days, I felt sorry for him. He almost seemed human."

"Huh." That had certainly *not* been my experience with Gene. I longed to ask for her help with him, but I was too afraid to speak out.

"Have you seen Colby's new girlfriend?" Daphne asked.

"I just met her."

She arched an eyebrow. "I've personally seen *all* of her. They were having sex in one of the private cabanas at the pool club the first day they met! We would've gotten thrown out if we didn't own the place!"

"What do you know about her?" I asked.

She grimaced. "Not much. She works fast, though. She hasn't even been around for a whole week, and she's already got her claws into Colby. He can't keep his hands off her. Olivia Jensen's having a fit, but Colby said he didn't care. He won't break up with her. He told me he was *serious* about her. Since when has he been serious about anything?"

"I don't know." I had an uneasy feeling about the

relationship, which just added to my big, fat pile of things to worry about at the moment.

"Anyway, I have to get going. See you tonight?" She hopped up, fit and sprightly as ever.

"Are we having dinner?"

Daphne tilted her head at me. "We're going to the Nguyen's for an end-of-the-summer soiree. Didn't Bryce tell you? Everyone's going to be there—including the Joneses. I better go pick out something to wear. Mimi Jones is going to be up my ass. See you!"

"Yes, see you," I said weakly. I hadn't been back on the island for an hour, and I was already overwhelmed. Dinner at Kelli and Kenji Nguyen's? With the Jones family, not to mention the rest of Mount Desert Island society? I'd only run out on my husband a week ago after brawling with Felicia Jones at that wedding... *Ugh!* Maybe Bryce wouldn't make me go. But Daphne sounded pretty sure of herself.

I quietly entered the house and crept along the corridor, eager to be alone in my room. Bryce was probably in his office on a call. The halls were blessedly silent, and I made it to the primary suite undetected. Inside, I closed the door and sank down onto the bed, inhaling the scent of Bryce's sheets. No matter what—no matter the price I'd eventually have to pay—it was good to be back.

My phone buzzed with a text from an unknown number.

Mr. Windsor has an urgent message for you. Click the below link.

I stared at the screen. Had I just said it was good to be back?

Obviously, I'd spoken too soon.

NINE

instructions

CHLOE

I DIDN'T IMMEDIATELY HIT the button. I sat on the bed, heart pounding, wondering what the hell I'd gotten myself into.

There was only one way to find out.

The link brought me to another video, but this time it was a well-dressed, dark-skinned woman with gray hair and designer eyeglasses who addressed me. "Good afternoon, Mrs. Windsor. I'm Attorney Finley, part of Gene Windsor's legal team. I want you to understand that I have attorney-client privilege with Mr. Windsor. I am acting on my client's behalf. As a result, I cannot be prosecuted or deemed in violation of any state or federal

laws, ordinances, or regulations as a result of this electronic transmission."

"Okay..."

But Attorney King talked over me—it was a prere-
corded message. "I also want to state that the opinions
and statements I am communicating via this message
are solely the opinions and statements of my client. I am
not legally responsible or liable for any of these opinions or statements. That being said, here is the message
from my client."

She looked straight into the screen. "You will attend
the Nguyen's party tonight. You will behave yourself—
no drinking, fighting, or contact with Felicia Jones. Not
so much as a scowl. You will dress appropriately and
stand by your husband's side all night."

She cleared her throat. "My client wants to know
who Colby's new girlfriend is. Talk to her, find out as
much information as possible, and meet with Olivia
Jensen first thing in the morning. He expects a full
report."

I wondered what Gene would think of the fact that
Tate was an escort. I didn't know if he knew about *me*...
Oh my goodness, this was getting complicated. My
head was spinning.

"There is one other thing," Attorney Finley continued. "It's imperative that you understand your place in

all of this. You are more my client's employee than you are his son's wife. That is the only reason he's allowed you to come back. You work for him, and you'd do well to remember that even though he's on the sidelines, he's still the one calling the plays."

The attorney blinked—she looked as if she was waking up from a Gene-Windsor-induced trance. "That's all, Mrs. Windsor. Please close this link and clear your search history. We'll be in touch again soon." The screen went blank.

I did as I was told, clearing out the search history and texting Olivia to make an early-morning appointment. She texted back immediately. *It's about time! I will also see you at the party tonight. Please wear something appropriate!*

My head thudded with the beginning of a headache. There was too much to consider. I lay down, trying to organize my thoughts.

Although he was "on the sidelines," Gene Windsor was still a considerable threat. He'd allowed me to come back, but now I was—for all intents and purposes— basically his bitch. I couldn't say no to him, and I couldn't tell Bryce the truth for fear of Gene retaliating: I was backed into a corner. Reporting on Colby's new "girlfriend" was one thing, but what else would Gene ask me to do?

Next on the list was the mysterious Tate. Who had hired her? If it wasn't Gene, the next obvious choice was Felicia Jones. But why would Bryce's ex hire an escort to infiltrate the Windsors? Was it just to torture me? Felicia certainly had the means to hire an investigator to learn more about me. But if she had, why now? And what was the goal?

I wanted to tell Bryce about Tate immediately, but again, she'd threatened to come out and tell the press the truth about me. I had my husband's reputation to think about. If Tate went public with the news that I'd worked for AccommoDating, it would irrevocably damage Bryce's position with the company.

Finally, I still needed to worry about my step-monster Lydia and my father. Gene had said they were already on his payroll. I had zero idea what they might do. They might be satisfied if they had enough money to stay in rent and booze. But Lydia was greedy and vindictive. She knew the Windsors were a goldmine; I had little hope that she'd be satisfied with a lifetime supply of boxed wine.

I pulled the covers up to my chin. How was it, I wondered, that I'd accumulated so many freaking enemies in such a short time?

But it wasn't really me that they were after—it was the Windsors' money, influence, and power. Bryce was the acting CEO of Windsor Enterprises now. He was a billionaire. Being married to him meant that I was somebody. Whereas before, as Chloe Burke of East Boston, people could've cared less whether I lived or died—my own father included. But being Bryce's wife meant that I had access to unlimited money, life-changing money.

Gene Windsor wanted to protect that money and control his family.

Lydia and my father wanted to get rich quick without lifting a finger.

And Tate the Escort wanted to make hay while the sun was shining, to rake in the cash while she could. As for who hired her, I would have to wait and see. If Felicia Jones was behind it, the motivation was probably to humiliate me. Or maybe she still wanted Bryce back...

The headache moved from dull to throbbing. *Ugh.* I had to get through the party tonight without any trouble, but all I wanted to do was pull the blankets up over my head and pretend I didn't exist.

I quieted my mind, focused on breathing, and tried to relax. I was caught in a web that had nothing to do with me. I was a pawn. I'd come to this place to be Bryce's wife—at the beginning of all this, I'd been hired to do a job. That had been difficult to begin with. *Bryce* had been difficult. But I couldn't lie to myself; despite all the turmoil swirling around me, I was relieved to be back in Maine. There was no place I'd rather be than with my husband. That was the truth.

I just had to make sure that I didn't do anything to hurt him.

Leaving had been bad, but now I feared that his father could make me do something worse. I had no idea what that was; I couldn't pretend to understand Gene Windsor's ultimate plan. It seemed to me that all he cared about was his company and his reputation, which was why he'd wanted me separated from Bryce in the first place.

So what did he want now—why the change of heart? And what would he ask of me?

I decided to approach the situation with Gene moment by moment. For now, I would go along with what he'd asked me to do. No one would be hurt by my reporting on Colby's new girlfriend, and nothing bad would come of me wearing an appropriate dress and staying by my husband's side all night.

But what if he asked me to do something worse?

I couldn't imagine what that might be, but again, I wouldn't put anything past Gene. He might get jealous of Bryce's position in the company and want to sabotage his own son. What would I do then?

I could never, ever hurt my husband... The problem was my brother. I shivered, remembering Gene's words. *"You have a lot to lose. When I say that, I'm not just thinking of your marriage. I'm thinking of your brother."*

I was Noah's family. I was all he had in the world. I *had* to protect him. That meant, for now, I couldn't tell Bryce the truth. And I didn't know when, or if, I'd be able to.

I scrunched my eyes shut and refused to think any further. I pulled the covers up, inhaling my husband's scent. *I'm safe for now. I'm with Bryce for now.*

But for how much longer?

peak

BRYCE

Regina Hernandez kept talking about the numbers, and the market, and the fallout, but I couldn't seem to focus. All I could think about was my wife.

My dick twitched beneath my suit.

I unmuted my microphone. "Excuse me. I've got another call that I'm going to have to take. Talk this afternoon?"

Regina blinked at me from the screen. She wasn't used to being interrupted. "I guess so."

"Great." I exited the video conference before she could press for details. It was suddenly Very Important that I find Chloe.

My dick twitched again. *Very fucking important.*

I took the stairs two at a time, almost knocking into one of the maids.

"Mr. Windsor!" She jumped out of my way.

"Sorry." But I wasn't sorry—I was impatient.

I barreled into our room and found Chloe wrapped underneath the covers, fast asleep. I locked the door behind me, watching her for a moment. Her long, thick hair spilled out over the pillow, and her beautiful face was peaceful in sleep, relaxed in a way I hadn't seen in a long time. Her full lips were slightly open as she breathed deeply.

My heart twisted at the sight of her. Being with Chloe had shown me something about myself, and it scared the shit out of me: I was capable of truly loving another person. The problem with that was that she could leave me again. She could leave me for good.

But I hoped that wouldn't happen; I knew she loved me, too. I could protect her. We could have a life together beyond even my wildest dreams. I'd always had the money, the houses, the ability to do whatever I wanted, buy whatever I wanted, and go wherever I wanted. But it had been an empty existence—and I'd only just realized it.

That realization happened in the most insane way possible.

My father had made it a condition of my trust that I

marry. I'd been so angry about that. I'd wanted *nothing* to fucking do with it after the shit Felicia put me through. I'd vowed to spend my life alone. But Gene hadn't allowed that. Even though he'd worked his way through several wives since my mother died, he still felt that being married legitimized a man. He believed as long as I was single, I was still a boy, too immature to take on a leadership role at Windsor Enterprises.

So I'd gone and shown him: I bought myself a wife.

At first I'd thought the idea of "buying" a bride was insane, but it suited my purposes. I hadn't wanted to get emotionally entangled with anyone, and I wanted control. In retrospect, I could see that I'd been kidding myself. Control was an illusion, a game of make-believe one played by oneself. Once you involved other people —once they became real to you—there was no controlling anything.

I stared at Chloe, her gorgeous face, which had become dear to me. I wanted her in a way I'd never wanted anybody before. I wanted to possess her, inside and out. I wanted to give myself to her, too.

My dick twitched again, growing uncomfortably hard beneath my clothes. *Speaking of losing control...*

I stripped out of my clothes and slid beneath the cool covers. I wrapped my arm around Chloe's warm body, and she nestled against me, making a happy sound when I kissed the top of her head. My heart twisted as I held her tight. I wanted her, but it was so much more than that. Chloe made me *happy*.

When had I ever been happy?

"Bryce?" She opened one eye, squinting at me.

"Who else would it be, huh?" I kissed her cheek and pulled her against me possessively, flexing my rock-hard cock against her soft skin.

She felt it because both eyes popped open, widening, and her cheeks started to flush. "I thought you were working."

"I'm always working." I flexed my hips and thrust against her. It felt so fucking good.

"Mmm." Chloe stripped out of her shirt and underwear without another word, all the better to press herself against me. I could already feel her wet heat calling to me. I didn't kiss her—not yet—I just enjoyed feeling the anticipation build between us, her body getting hotter by the second, her pupils dilating as she looked up at me in breathless anticipation.

Fuck, I loved it when she looked at me like that—like I could make all of her dreams come true.

I intended to start now. I lowered my lips to hers, brushing them lightly against each other, my cock so hard and dripping that I already felt like I might burst. I forced myself to take it slow. I ran my hands down her sides, her back, her stomach, her thighs, then finally to her breasts. I took each mound in my hand and gently caressed them, increasing the pressure as Chloe arched her back, leaning into me. She loved it when I played with her tits. Her eagerness turned me on, so I bent down and sucked on each nipple, nipping and lapping, blowing cold air on them until she was writhing and squirming beneath me. Each tender bud stood at erect attention.

She clung to me, trying to angle my dick toward her entrance.

I laughed. "Not so fast." As if *she* was the only eager one, the only one about to lose it if I didn't get inside her. Again, control was an illusion, but I deluded myself for a few moments longer to stretch out her pleasure. I dipped my hand between her thighs, my fingers coated in wetness. She was so, so ready for me.

Once I got in there, I was going to fucking lose it.

Chloe had been a virgin when I first took her, a fact that made my chest bloom with hot pride. She was mine and mine forever. She got wet for *me*. It was *my* dick she craved, that she whimpered for.

I inserted the head of my cock at her entrance, and she moaned. "Please, Bryce."

She would never be with anyone but me. I fucking *owned* her, and I was going to show her right now. The fact that she'd left me... *Fuck.* It made me crazy to think about it, that she'd gone away and might never have come back...

I inched myself inside her, and she cried out, clamping herself around me, her face transformed in ecstasy. I flexed my hips, getting a rhythm going, forcing myself to take it slow so I didn't hurt her and come in one second. She was so wet, so fucking *tight.* Her pussy squeezed me, making me see double. *Fuck!*

I stopped for a second, so I didn't lose it right then.

Breathing hard, Chloe snapped her eyes open. She'd already been lost in the moment. "What's the matter?" she panted.

"I just needed a second." I smiled at her, even though I was raging inside. Raging to take her, raging that she'd left me, raging that I was going to mark her so deep she would never try to abandon me again.

She smiled back, and it was like the sun coming out. Her eyes were clear and her gaze was direct; she looked genuinely happy. "I love you."

I melted inside, my fears washing away. She healed me. Being inside her, being one with her, healed me. Nothing could be more perfect. "I love you, too."

Laughing, she grabbed my ass cheeks. "Then give

me what I want, Mr. Windsor." She ground herself against my shaft.

Fuck. I didn't hesitate—I couldn't. I thrust into her all the way, and we both cried out.

Chloe dug her nails into my ass as I drove into her. I could not stop myself, my long strokes going deeper into her wet, tight heat.

"I love you," I said again; I needed her to know I felt it, especially once I was inside her. I felt so connected to my wife, so complete. I let my body take over, leaning up on my arms and thrusting all the way in. Chloe writhed beneath me and gripped my ass, urging me deeper inside each time *Fuck.* There was nothing else like this.

She squeezed herself around my cock, arching her back and grinding against the base of my shaft. I almost lost it, but I pulled all the way out, waiting, knowing I was so close—until Chloe begged me to fill her again, whimpering and pleading. I waited until we were both shaking, hot with anticipation and need.

And then I slammed all the way into her.

"Bryce!" Chloe shattered beneath me, her pussy gripping me, urging me on. Time stopped as her spasms enveloped me, and I started to come, relentlessly driving deep. Our orgasms shook the bed as I exploded inside her. Chloe clawed my back and came again, which drove me out of my fucking mind.

I lost myself, hips flexing, grunting, out of my goddamned mind. I finally came to rest, careful not to crush her.

At the same time, we both turned to each other and smiled.

"That was…" Chloe didn't finish the sentence.

"Yeah." I was beyond words, but I found the ones I needed to say before I passed out. "I love you, Mrs. Windsor."

She nestled against me. "I love you, too."

I pulled her onto my chest, utterly spent and completely at peace. Only my wife could give me such a release—the combination of physical pleasure and knowing that I was safe, that I was loved.

I'd been born into wealth.

But for the first time in my life, I truly felt rich.

meeting

CHLOE

THE LAST THING I wanted to do was leave the bed to go to one of the Nguyen's parties, but I had little choice. Bryce made it easier because he had to take another call. He kissed me on the cheek, told me he loved me again and was gone. Once he left, the bed seemed cold.

I dragged myself up and into the shower. The luxurious bathroom and its designer personal-care items always cheered me, mainly because all the shampoo and shower gels smelled like Bryce. I lathered myself in every substance available, thinking about our encounter that afternoon. *Unf.* My husband was giving me all the attention I craved. I only wanted to be with him, to be next to him, to soak up as much of his love and presence as I could. It was like I was a lizard, and he was the sun: I had to take as much as I could get because I would need it later.

Later, if I had to leave him again.

I shoved the thought from my mind. Maybe Gene would let me stay. Perhaps he'd agree that keeping things on an even keel would benefit his son and, more importantly to Gene, his company. I would just have to try and convince him.

For now, I vowed to bask in the warmth of Bryce's love and attention. I was helpless against it, anyway. I craved my husband—his touch, his approval, his presence. I intended to get it while the getting was good.

I rough-dried my hair and left my face bare: Midge would want to be in charge of my appearance tonight. I hustled to the dressing room, formerly my bedroom, and found her inside having a whispered conversation.

With Hazel.

"Oh—hi!" I tightened my fluffy bathrobe against me. "I didn't expect you both to be in here."

Hazel and Midge turned to me. Midge's cheeks were flushed; Hazel's features were stony.

I'd obviously interrupted. "Is something wrong? I can come back—"

"No, Mrs. Windsor, I don't mean to cause a delay. You need to get ready for the party," Hazel said stiffly.

"Midge and I were just discussing something. We could use your help."

Midge's nostrils flared. "*I* didn't agree to that! You think it's a good idea, but I don't. Chloe has enough on her plate at the moment."

"*Mrs. Windsor,*" Hazel corrected her, "can most likely make a decision for herself. Can't you, Mrs. Windsor?"

"A decision about what?"

"Ugh, we don't have time for this! Chloe has to get ready for the party." Midge flew to the wardrobe and started going through the racks of dresses.

"I can talk to *Mrs. Windsor* while you dress her." Hazel glanced at me, arching a penciled-in eyebrow. "Is that acceptable to you?"

Hazel scared me, but I knew one thing: she was loyal to my husband. "You helped me when I needed it." I was reminding her as much as myself about the night she helped me and Noah get off the island. "I'm listening."

The maid nodded. "Midge and I were just discussing the fact that things have been very tumultuous for the family of late."

"It's true." Midge held up a tangerine-colored dress and frowned at it. "A lot of crazy shit's been going on."

Hazel's eyebrow arched impossibly higher. "That's crude language, young lady. We do not speak like that in front of the family!"

"Oops." Midge didn't look too worried, though—she looked more concerned about the next dress she pulled, a forest-green one with a high neckline. "They want you in something demure tonight, but I swear to God, these are some of the ugliest dresses I've ever seen in my life."

Hazel rolled her eyes and turned back to me. "While Midge secures a dress, I'd like to ask for your help with something. It's about Colby's new...lady-friend."

Midge snorted. "Calling her a lady's a little much, don't you think?"

"I think we can proceed without any more of your comments."

Midge rolled her eyes and kept tearing through the dresses.

"We have some concerns about his new friend Tate. She's only been here for a few days, but there have already been several incidents." Hazel pursed her lips.

I sank down onto the bed. "Daphne mentioned something about the pool club."

Hazel nodded. "The manager called here to complain that they'd been having loud...relations...in one of the cabanas."

"Not to mention what they were doing on the beach this afternoon!" Midge added. "And in the woods! In *broad daylight*! The elder Mr. Windsor just got arrested—we can't have that sort of thing going on with the photographers still sneaking around. Olivia Jensen's about to have a fit."

"Olivia's spoken to both Colby and Tate, but Colby doesn't see a problem," Hazel said. "The girl seems completely reckless. That's why we wanted to speak with you."

"That's why *you* wanted to speak with her." Midge pulled out a flowing yellow dress. "*I* wanted to give her a break. She just got back. Things have been crazy."

Hazel turned to me. "I did want to speak with you because I thought that, as the lady of the house, you might talk some sense into her."

"Isn't Daphne the lady of the house?" I asked.

Her nostrils flared. "The other Mrs. Windsor isn't exactly a paradigm of reputable behavior."

That was probably the truth. Daphne *had* cheated with Micheal Jones in public, out by the bonfire at the benefit dinner we'd hosted... "What can I do to help?"

"Talk to her," Hazel said. "Explain that this is a difficult time for the family. Maybe say that you appreciate that she and Colby are enjoying each other but that they need to be more discreet about it."

"She might think I don't have much room to talk." My cheeks heated, remembering the time Bryce and I had sex in a dressing room in Northeast Harbor.

"But you and Mr. Windsor are married. Being a newlywed's different from being..."

"A flavor of the week." Midge approached with the yellow dress and a pair of gold-toned sandals. She held the dress up against me, then nodded her approval. "You'll look beautiful in this. *And* it's demure."

"It's pretty," I said.

She eyed my hair. "We need to deal with that before it dries more. Into the makeup chair, Mrs. Windsor." She winked at Hazel. "You wanna say anything else?"

Hazel sighed. "Not particularly. But Mrs. Windsor, will you please update us? All of the staff feels strongly that this situation must be dealt with before the family has to endure more bad press."

"Of course, Hazel. I'll talk to her tonight—she might not listen, though."

She nodded. "I appreciate it." She clicked to the door, her spindly little legs carrying her quickly from the room.

"Sheesh, she's a pain in the ass." Midge stuffed me into the makeup chair and whipped out the blow dryer. "She doesn't take no for an answer."

"She *is* loyal to the family, though."

"True, and I admire her for that." Midge started brushing out my hair. "But I thought it was a big ask for us to come to you about this. You just got back."

"I'm surprised Hazel asked me." Actually, I was somewhat flattered. "I just don't know if I can help."

Midge nodded. "I think this girl's real trouble. Chef caught her stuffing food and a couple of bottles of expensive wine into her bag. Like she was stealing, you know? He told her she could have whatever she wanted, but she acted super defensive about it."

"Maybe she's not used to being able to have nice things." I could certainly relate to that. "But all the public...relations...is a problem. I can't be having that around my brother. And Hazel's right, we don't need any more scandals now. I'll try talking to her."

In turn, Tate would probably threaten me again—or worse—but maybe I could talk some sense into her. If Colby was genuinely taken with her, maybe there could be a real future for them. Selfishly, I hoped not, but maybe Tate wasn't as bad as she seemed.

"Enough about her—how are *you*? How was the trip? Your skin is glowing, so I'm taking it as a good sign. That and all the hollering I heard coming from down the hall this afternoon." She laughed.

"Ugh!" My cheeks burned. "Sorry about that."

"Why, girl? I'm not! I'm so glad you're back and that you and Mr. Windsor are happy again. He's *impossible* when you're not around. Chef said he didn't eat once. Hazel said he barely slept. He was snappy with the staff. He needs you, Chloe—*we* need you. It's been so crazy with the arrest and all. Can you even believe it? Gene Windsor's in *prison*. I can't picture him in there with the other inmates, you know what I mean?"

"I can't either," I admitted. "I wonder what's going to happen."

Midge's eyes grew wide as she fired up the blow dryer. "He might not come back." That was all she could say as she started to dry my hair.

Over the roar of the dryer, I could say nothing in return.

But was it awful that I hoped she was right?

the stage

CHLOE

"WELL, DON'T YOU LOOK PRETTY." Bryce waited for me at the bottom of the stairs.

"Thank you. You look handsome like always." My husband wore a dark suit, blue dress shirt, and blue tie. He looked every inch the billionaire CEO. Bryce held out his big hand for me, and I shivered as I took it, remembering how his hands had roamed down my naked body only hours before...

"Don't look at me like that," he growled. "Otherwise I'll throw you over my shoulder and take you back upstairs."

I fought the urge to fan myself. "Okay."

"Chloe, *stop*. We have to go out tonight. Don't give

me blue-balls before we even leave the house." He pulled me close, and I could feel an erection already stirring.

"Stop," I admonished, but I didn't mean it. I'd love for Bryce to drag me back upstairs and have his way with me again!

"Hey, guys!" Colby strolled in with Tate glued to his side. A pissed-looking Jake trailed behind them.

Jake Windsor was the middle child, tall and handsome like his brothers. He looked a lot like Bryce but had a more narrow face, hazel eyes, and lighter hair. His scowl looked like Bryce's, though.

"Hey, Jake. I haven't seen you." I hugged my brother-in-law.

Jake gave me a quick smile. "I'm glad you're back. We missed you."

I blushed with pleasure. "Thanks."

As soon as I stepped back, his scowl returned. The reason for this became immediately apparent. Colby had his hand on Tate's ass, rubbing it. She was snuggled up against him, batting her long lashes. The vibe between them was so sexy it felt uncomfortable to witness, inappropriate for company. I should know! Bryce and I had at least stepped away from each other before his burgeoning erection had taken center stage.

Colby and Tate were so busy making goo-goo eyes

at each other that they didn't bother saying anything else to the rest of us.

"Hey, little brother." Bryce raised his eyebrows. "Hey, Tate."

"Hi." She tore herself away from eye-fucking Colby long enough to grace my husband with a megawatt smile.

"Hey, Bryce." Colby grinned at him, hand never leaving Tate's ample backside. "You guys ready for this party?"

"Not yet—can I speak with you for a moment? You too, Jake." Bryce turned to me. "This'll just take a second."

"Sure." I nodded.

"No problem!" Tate said brightly, her eyes trailing appreciatively over Bryce's muscled form.

I counted backward from ten. If I lost it on her—and got into yet *another* fight—Gene Windsor would have my head on a platter.

Once the men were gone, she tossed her long blond hair over her shoulder and gave my dress a once-over. "You look like a grandma."

The yellow dress Midge had chosen was long, flowing, and had a high neckline. I had to admit that it was more my style than the sexy dresses she usually chose. "Tell me how you really feel, Tate."

"I just did." She gave me another blinding, fake smile, and I again fought the urge to smack her.

"You look...nice." The truth was, Tate looked exactly like what she was—a high-end escort. Her one-shoulder black jumpsuit was skintight, showing off her trim figure and killer curves. Her sky-high heels would be out of place on the Nguyen's rolling lawn, but they made her butt stick out—which Colby had definitely appreciated. "Listen, I've been wanting to talk to you. I've heard a couple of things from the staff."

Tate's nostril flared. "Is this about that stupid Mexican chef? He accused me of *stealing*! Can you imagine that? I just wanted some snacks and wine for my room!"

"Woah, okay. First of all, he's Spanish, not Mexican. Second of all, no, that's not what I was talking about. It's more about how you and Colby have been getting... close...in various public places." I took a deep breath. "It's making people uncomfortable, Tate. My little brother lives here, you know? I can't have him seeing something like that."

"Just because you dress like a grandma and don't have sex with your husband doesn't mean you get to be the morality police with *me*." She puffed her chest out. "What Colby and I do is our business. He's a Windsor too, remember? This is his home, his island, his all of it.

If he can't keep his hands off me, that isn't anybody's business."

"First of all, it's not actually his home—it's Bryce's. Second of all, you're right: it *isn't* anybody's business what you guys do with each other. That's the whole point! There's staff around, family, little kids, and there's still paparazzi—"

"Did someone say paparazzi? Aw, my favorite topic!" Olivia Jensen strolled in, her fiery-red hair cascading in waves down her emerald-colored dress. I hadn't seen the PR executive since I'd been back. She looked as lovely and poised as ever, and also, as laser-focused.

She eyed Tate up and down, her perfectly groomed eyebrows arching slightly. "That's an outfit," she said by way of a greeting.

"Oh hey, if it isn't the actual morality police." Tate snorted. "Who invited *you*?"

"You two have met?" I looked between Tate and Olivia. They were now openly glaring at each other.

Wow, this was going to be a fun night.

"We've met several times. Haven't we, Tate?" Olivia gave her a final once-over before turning back to me. "It's nice to see you, Chloe. You look great."

"Thank you." I didn't miss Tate's eye roll. I hoped

Olivia could help me talk some sense into her. "We were just discussing the fact that the paparazzi are still watching the island. I was telling Tate that we need to be careful about how we act when we're out in public. Even just outside the house." I flushed, remembering how the press had followed Bryce and me out into the island woods, catching us during some very private moments...

"Funny, Tate and I have had the same conversation repeatedly." Olivia straightened her shoulders. "I've explained that the Windsor family is on a press detox, as I like to call it. We must be vigilant about every image we present to the world."

"Why do I feel singled out?" Tate motioned to me. "Mike Tyson here's the one who just threw down at that wedding. All I've done is make out with my new boyfriend."

Olivia threw up her hands. "The staff at the pool club said you were screaming your *head* off in one of the cabanas—"

"Hey, Olivia." Colby ambled out and protectively put his arm around Tate. "Everything okay?"

"Not really," Olivia said, direct as usual. "Chloe and I were just explaining to Tate that this is a delicate time for the family because of Gene's arrest. We all need to be cognizant of the roles we have to play. We need to build trust in the family name again. I have a couple of guys who will be taking photos tonight—we need to present a unified front. The board's been up my derriere, so to speak, about cleaning up the family image."

"I understand," Colby said quickly. "Bryce and I were just talking about it." He turned to Tate. "We're going to grab you a jacket to wear, okay? I think you look great, but Bryce wants us to be super conservative because they think it'll help the business. Okay, babe?"

"Sure, babe." She looked up at him and nodded, eyes wide, as if he were a king and she was his most loyal subject. "Whatever you think is best."

"Great." He kissed the tip of her nose, and they strode off, arms wrapped around each other, without further argument.

"That was easier than I thought." I eyed Olivia, who was still watching them. "That should make it better, right?"

She sighed as she turned back to me. "Not really. Colby was under strict instructions not to start seeing someone until things quieted down around here. The fact that he met this girl and she's practically living with him three days later is a red flag. Not to mention all the other red flags, like the fact that she's completely two-faced and already has his balls in her back pocket."

I grimaced. "Yeah, there's definitely a red flag or two." *Like the fact that she's an escort and Colby doesn't know it. And also, she's threatened to blackmail me.* Just a few minor details!

Olivia forced a smile. "How about you, huh? Are you happy to be back? I know we're scheduled to chat tomorrow, but I'd love to know how everything's going. Are things settled down between you and Bryce?"

"Yes. And I'm sorry about how I left. I was having a hard time." I grimaced. It was hitting me that we had to go to this party and that everyone would be talking about me and the fact that I'd fought Felicia Jones. "But yes, things are settled and good."

"So, are you staying? And are you planning on any more fights?" Olivia Jensen didn't beat around the bush too much.

"Yes I'm staying, and no, I don't plan on any more fighting." I raised my chin. "That sort of behavior's behind me now. I'm going to stay with Bryce tonight, and no tequila, I promise."

"Great." But Olivia grimaced. "As you can tell with Tate, the old PR adage is true: there's always another fire to put out. Help me if you can, okay? Tate's a handful. And I thought Daphne was bad!"

~

The party was in full swing by the time we arrived. Twinkle lights glittered from the nearby trees, a string quartet played instrumental love songs in the background, and the enormous banquet table was decorated with vases bursting with fresh local flowers. As always, the sky above Mount Desert Island was the real showstopper, blanketed with stars as far as the eye could see.

Well-dressed guests dotted the lawn, sipping cocktails and gossiping. One thing I'd learned since I'd married Bryce? Rich people loved to get dressed up for each other. You'd think that the small group of wealthy islanders would tire of the same parties night after night. Still, judging by how harried the waitstaff and bartenders appeared, no one seemed to be ready to end the non-stop party season just yet.

Kelli and Kenji Nguyen greeted us warmly. They were a bi-coastal power couple, dividing their time between California and Maine; Kenji was in real estate, and Kelli was a Hollywood executive. I hadn't seen them since the wedding, but they were well-bred enough to not mention anything about the fight. Kenji started asking Bryce about business. Kelli leaned in for a hug, enveloping me in a mix of her toned arms and tawny hair.

"I was worried about you, Chloe. Are you doing better?" She kept her voice low.

I hugged her back. Kelli had always been kind to me. "Yes—thank you."

"I had to invite the Jones family tonight, of course. So Felicia's here." Kelli pulled back and inspected me. "Are you okay with that?"

"I'm not going to fight her if that's what you mean." I smiled, putting on a brave face. "Is she here with Finn Ryder?" Felicia had been dating a British guy from a band, and she'd seemed pretty happy with him—a massive relief for me. Bitch had finally stopped texting my husband!

"He's on tour, but from what I hear, they're still dating. So that's good." Kelli tilted her head toward the bar. "She's over there with her parents."

Mimi, Michael, and Felicia Jones were indeed at the bar. I watched as Mimi drained her glass, then held it out for a refill. "Ugh, her drinking has been so intense ever since she found out about Michael's affair." Kelli peered past me at Daphne, glowing and resplendent in a patterned, multicolored dress. "I hope there isn't a scene tonight. I heard Daphne's looking for a huge payday."

I watched as Mimi Jones knocked back another martini. "You might want to close the bar down."

Kelli followed my stare. "Oh boy. Let me see if I can

get them to water down the vodka." She hustled off toward the bar.

Daphne was immediately by my side. "Mimi's getting sloppy, huh? Michael won't look at me, of course. He's probably sweating bullets about telling his wife how much money he's going to have to cough up for this baby. And Felicia's giving you a death stare, FYI."

"Great." Why the hell had I come to this party?

"Ooh, by the way, I heard you and Olivia tried to talk some sense into Tate. Do you think it helped?"

We glanced over and saw Colby spoon-feeding Tate some sort of mousse canapé. She licked her lips suggestively and stared up at him with fuck-me eyes.

"Maybe not so much." I grimaced.

"Oh boy—here comes Bryce. I better move over. You're supposed to be next to him all night, right?" Daphne winked at me and hustled away.

"Right." Gene Windsor had been crystal-clear that I was to stand by my husband and stay out of trouble all night.

But...how the hell did Daphne know about that?

Before I could ponder it further, Bryce was at my side. I smiled at the man I loved, vowing to do what Gene asked.

I didn't know what would happen if I played my cards right.

But I knew exactly what would befall me if I played them wrong.

nobody

CHLOE

NOT LOOKING at Felicia Jones all night proved a true test of will. There was something about her—her blue, blue eyes, long, dark hair, and sparkling complexion were hard to look away from. The smattering of freckles across her nose, so unexpected, mesmerized. I could understand, at least from a distance, why Bryce had been taken with her.

When she shot daggers at me with her eyes, I sighed. I could also see why he was happy he never married her!

Bryce caught the nasty expression on Felicia's face as she glanced our way from the bar. He sighed. "Don't let her get to you. She's just upset that you kicked her ass."

Bryce chuckled, then wrapped his arms around me. "Let's just stand here and look happy, okay? That's the good press I need to start my first week as CEO off right."

"I'm so excited for you." With all the drama going on, I'd almost forgotten that this was Bryce's first *real* week as CEO. "What's happening? What's your agenda like?"

"You mean, besides trying to keep our shares from tanking, our stockholders from staging a mutiny, and my father's arrest from eclipsing everything we've worked to build as a company? You know, not much." He laughed.

"Babe, I'm sorry you're dealing with so much." I wrapped my arms around his waist, staring up at him. "You've been so good to me, taking me away for the weekend and making sure that Noah was settled back at the house."

"You mean kidnapping you and dragging you out of the country against your will." He arched an eyebrow.

"You say 'kidnapping,' I say 'taking.' I mean, I guess I was the one who originally said kidnapping because that's what happened. But it all worked out for the best." I grinned up at him. "The point is, I'm back. *We're* back. And I really want to support you right now."

"I appreciate that." He brushed the hair back from my face. "I might want you to come to Boston with me later in the week. I should make an appearance at headquarters. It would be good if you could be seen with me in the city. We can stay at my building; you'll love it."

"Building?"

He raised an eyebrow. "I own a townhouse in Beacon Hill. Didn't you know that?"

I raised *my* eyebrow. "No. I stayed at the Stratum, remember?"

"Ah yes, I remember," he growled, pulling me closer. "You'll like my townhouse better—one of the suites has a huge shower with a bench that'd be just *perfect* to bend you over." He playfully smacked my ass.

"Bryce." I shook my head. "We're supposed to be appropriate, remember? Demure."

"I don't know what 'demure' means, but if it has something to do with that dress, I'm all for it." He grinned down at me. "I intend to rip that off you later."

I shivered. "It's a date."

"Oh boy." Bryce took a step back. "Here comes trouble."

Jake ambled over to us, bourbon in hand. He still looked upset.

"What's up, little brother?" Bryce asked. "I thought the talk we gave Colby earlier was good, but you don't look happy."

"Why is it that he always gets away with murder? Dad would be up my ass if I violated Olivia's direct orders, but Colby's just having a good old time, as usual." He pointed across the party, where Colby and Tate were drinking, dancing, and laughing. They seemed to be in their own world. "I know Dad's aware of the situation. Has he even *said* anything?"

"He's probably too busy securing the top bunk and bribing as many prisoners as possible, so they protect him," Bryce said. "Plus, Dad never seems to worry about Colby much. They have a different relationship."

I longed to tell them that Gene was interested in Tate's relationship with his youngest son. But again, I said nothing. I felt crappy about it and like I was being dishonest because I was hiding something.

Because I *was* being dishonest. I *was* hiding something. I hated lying; I hated the position Gene had put me in.

"It's not just that." Jake sighed. "I'm feeling really stressed about getting more involved in the business. I'm not sure how to handle the team in Malaysia. I haven't worked with them before."

Bryce and Jake started talking about their global

operations, and I took the opportunity to head to the ladies' room. I made sure that Felicia was occupied first. She was engrossed in conversation with Kenji and another man I didn't recognize thank goodness. The last time I'd run into her in the bathroom, she'd been nasty, calling me a decoy and just generally being a total bitch. I should've fought her then!

Thinking about fighting Felicia, I cracked my knuckles as I headed to the Nguyen's "bathroom." It was a converted barn bigger than my apartment back in East Boston and about fifty times as pleasant. It seemed empty until one of the bathroom doors opened, and a visibly drunk Mimi Jones staggered out.

I did not have the best of luck in this bathroom.

"Hi, Mimi." I pretended to fix my hair so that I didn't look at her, didn't notice the stumble-step she took toward the sinks.

"Hello." Drunk as she was, she still managed to stick her nose up in the air. Mimi Jones was a beautiful woman, tanned, tall, and lean, with long legs, silky-smooth hair, and not a wrinkle in sight. They said money couldn't buy happiness, but it could definitely buy a good plastic surgeon! Still, for all her beauty and wealth, Mimi had sour energy. It hadn't helped that since she'd found out about her husband and Daphne, she'd doused herself in vodka.

She chose the sink next to me, causing me to take a step back. "I didn't think you'd be here," she sniffed.

"I didn't want to be here," I admitted. "But Kelli and Kenji are good friends of the family, and I wanted to support them."

"Ha! You sound so *proper*. That's a joke." She slurred her words slightly, so it came out *Thass a hoke*.

I started backing away—I didn't need to pee *that* bad. "I'll just leave you to it, have a good night—"

"Oh no, you don't." She whirled on me and almost fell over, but a true pro, Mimi recovered quickly. "You owe me, young lady. You're going to pay for what you did to my Felicia."

I sighed. "I'm sorry I went after her at the wedding. In my defense, she *was* messaging Bryce non-stop after we got married. It was inappropriate. She crossed a line, Mrs. Jones."

"*She* crossed a line? How about your *mother-in-law*, huh? Having sex with my husband, trying to steal him away from his family, getting pregnant on purpose, and then demanding an outrageous amount of money for child support?" Mimi's pretty face was pulled so tight she couldn't really scowl, but I sensed she was trying. "I think it's about time the Windsors got what they deserve."

"Gene's in prison," I reminded her. "And your husband's with you, not Daphne."

She snorted. "Lucky me!"

I headed for the exit, but she grabbed my wrist, yanking me back. "Ow!"

"Like I said, *no, you don't*," she hissed. "I'm not done with you."

I stood still. For all her proper clothes and immaculate blowout, Mimi Jones was pretty scary. She was also surprisingly strong.

"I know who you are, Chloe Burke." She gave me a triumphant, if hammered, smile. "I know where you came from and all about your little arrangement. That's what money can do, dear. It opens all sorts of doors. Nothing can hide from real wealth."

I felt as though she'd smacked me. "I don't know what you're talking about," I mumbled.

"Just stop—I know everything." Her eyes glittered with a mixture of vodka and triumph. "So you better be *very careful* about what you do. Come near my daughter again, I'll expose you for the whore you are. And if my Felicia wants Bryce back, she can have him."

I gaped at her. "He's my *husband*—"

"Like I said, quit your whining!" Mimi took a step toward me, and I promptly took a step back.

"Right now she's lusting over that silly Finn, but

she'll come to her senses. She and Bryce were meant to be. They stand to inherit Windsor Enterprises and *all* of Gene's money—including my husband's payout to Daphne. It's all going to come back to me in the end." She tried to wink at me, but it came off as more of a blink. "So you stay away from my daughter. Stay out of her way and remember—you're a nobody. I can ruin you in an instant, and I won't think twice about it."

She strode past me. Even though she wobbled a bit, she seemed damn sure of herself.

Heart thudding in my chest, I watched her go.

I turned back to my reflection in the mirror; I looked pale with shock. *Mimi Jones knows about me.* She knew I worked for the escort agency. She knew that my marriage was fake, at least in the beginning.

My whole life—Bryce's entire life—could be blown up in an instant.

I was surrounded by enemies, people who hated me, and people who viewed me as a nuisance. I was nothing more than a prop, something they could use to get what they wanted.

Mimi's words rang in my ear. *You're a nobody.*

I felt sick inside, but I couldn't even shed a tear.

Nobodies didn't cry.

sure

CHLOE

BRYCE WAS INCREDIBLY BUSY. As the new acting CEO, he had more authority, responsibilities, and legitimacy within the company. Because Windsor Enterprises had operations around the globe, Bryce was in meetings at all hours of the day and night. He barely slept. When I saw him, I kissed him, babied him, and admonished him to eat healthily and take care of himself.

"I miss you," he grumbled. "We're going to Boston Wednesday night. I'll have to work over the weekend, but I'm taking enough of a break so that we can spend some time together."

"Sounds great. But remember, I'm right here." I leaned up and gave him a hug. "You can always work from the bed, you know. I'll snuggle up next to you and won't say a word."

"Like I'd be able to concentrate." He pulled me close, and the familiar heat kicked up between us. "Mmm. I have to go." With another quick kiss, he pulled away, off to meet with the board and ensure the pending charges against his father didn't implode the business.

I missed him, but it was good that my husband was occupied. Being Gene Windsor's bitch kept me on my toes.

I had a lot to do.

First up was my meeting with Olivia Jensen. Even though it was early in the morning after the Nguyen's party, she was dressed in a blue silk blouse, her hair and makeup impossibly perfect. "I understand that Gene asked you to find out more about Tate. So." She leaned over her desk. "What do you know?"

"Not much more than you," I lied. I'd tossed and turned all night, my head full of Mimi Jones's threats, mixed with worries about what to report about Tate. I couldn't tell Olivia the truth about her being an escort. That would blow up in my face, and there was already too much about to ignite in my world.

"Will you speak to Gene directly?" I asked. I was curious about Olivia's actual relationship with her billionaire-mogul client. Did she know that he was basically blackmailing me?

"No, I won't see him for at least another week—his visitor list hasn't been approved yet. I'm preparing notes for his lawyers, and they'll pass them along." She fired up her laptop and started tapping away. "He's indicated through the firm that he thought you would be a good point of contact for Tate because you guys are roughly the same age. But she didn't seem too friendly toward you last night."

I shook my head. "She doesn't like me very much. The staff asked me to talk to her about her behavior, but she just got defensive. When I first met her, she only told me a little bit. She's from Boston, the South End, and she met Colby at the pool club. Also, Chef caught her taking a bunch of wine and food from the kitchen. She yelled at him and was super rude about it."

"So she's not used to being around all this." Olivia motioned to the house.

"It seems like that. She's a little rough around the edges."

Olivia sighed. "Does it bother anyone besides me that she came out of nowhere? MDI is a small community. Everyone knows everyone. But I can't find one person from the club who knows who she is. You have to be on a guest list, they don't just let you in there."

"I'll ask her if that helps," I offered.

"Thank you." Olivia tapped some more on the keyboard. "This whole thing worries me— Colby seems out of his mind. There's been a lot of inappropriate behavior, and it's been *very* quick and intense. I know he's a big boy, but he seems over his head with this girl."

"I agree. I wonder what it is about her..."

Olivia frowned. "I know he's always had a soft spot for strippers—maybe since she doesn't come from a lot, he feels sorry for her."

"I don't know if he feels sorry." In fact, the only thing I'd seen him feeling was Tate *up* on the boat ride home from the party. "But Colby's a good guy. If he sees something in her, maybe she's not as bad as we think."

Olivia's lip curled. "Unfortunately, that's not usually how this works. Can you talk to her some more and see if you can find out anything else? In the meantime, I'll let Gene know you've been helpful."

"Thanks." I meant it. If Gene was satisfied, it meant I got more time with Bryce.

I'd take whatever I could get.

The following two days passed without incident. No one threatened to blackmail me. Gene didn't send me any video messages; he was quiet from the confines of his jail cell. Mimi Jones didn't get drunk and accost me, Felicia Jones was busy doing god-knows-what, Daphne was off-island shopping, and Tate and Colby were nowhere to be seen. Midge said she'd heard they'd been barricaded in the guesthouse having nonstop sex. At least they'd gone someplace private! Maybe Tate was getting the message, after all.

Still, the relative calm unnerved me. It felt like the island was holding its breath, just waiting for the next round of drama to unleash havoc on all of us.

The only new pictures of the Windsor family on the internet were from the Nguyen's party. The photos were mainly of Bryce and me, and the details were about who'd designed my dress. One stray headline posed the question: *Chloe's Back—is Brylecia Done for Good?* "Brylecia" was the press's pet name for Bryce and Felicia, so I freaking hoped so!

Gene Windsor had instructed me to stay away from her so things looked better for the family—more settled, calmer. So far, it had been working. I prayed my good behavior kept my father-in-law satisfied.

Other items needing my attention were Elena and Akira. When I'd been in trouble, they were the first two people I called. But as soon as I'd returned to Bryce I'd been quiet, except for my questions about Tate. I'd probably given them whiplash with so much back and forth over the past few months.

My lawyer was snippy with me. "I can't believe it's back on with him just like that. You told me you wanted out."

"You told me I should go back," I reminded her.

"*I* told you to not sign the contract in the first place! Remember that?"

"Of course, I remember. I'm sorry—I've been all over the place, I admit it." I sighed. "I'm just glad you're still taking my calls."

"You're still my client." Akira's tone softened a little. "And I charge for telephone calls, remember?"

I laughed. "Then we should talk business for a second. Did Noah's guardianship papers go through yet?"

My father had signed another agreement waiving his rights to Noah in exchange for even more money. We'd filed it with the court immediately thereafter. But if the judge hadn't approved it yet, there still a chance he and Lydia could make a legal claim for my brother's return.

"It hasn't been approved yet. The family court's insanely backed up. But it *should* go through—as long as

Bryce isn't trying to take him from you anymore." Akira wasn't about to let me forget about Bryce's ugly threats.

I winced. "Of course not."

"No, of *course* not."

I hesitated for a moment. "Akira...are you mad at me for going back to him?"

"No Chloe, I'm *worried* about you. Some of the things you're doing don't seem like you. You took this job because you needed the money and to get Noah away from a bad situation. But then you ran away from Bryce in the middle of the night like you were scared of something—something you haven't shared with me. And then you ran right back to him two minutes after telling me you wanted out of the contract." She went quiet for a moment. "Like I said, I'm worried about you. It seems like there's more going on here than you're sharing with me."

"I can't... I can't talk about it." I shook my head.

"I'm your lawyer. You can tell me anything and it's confidential, so long as it's not in an attempt to commit or cover up a crime or fraud." When I didn't speak, she sighed again. "Call me if you want to talk, okay? I'm here for you."

Once she'd hung up, I stared off into space. The reason I *hadn't* confided in Akira wasn't that I was worried about being prosecuted. It was because I feared

Gene Windsor. He'd told me to keep our arrangement a secret, and he'd threatened me. He was just scary enough for me to believe he'd follow through. I'd love to know if she could help me with that situation, but it seemed too dangerous.

It was best to keep my own counsel.

I called Elena next. "Please don't tell me you quit or got fired again," she said. "I just put a deposit down on a private school. *Non-refundable.*"

"No, it's nothing like that. I was just wondering... Do you have any peers down there? Like, anyone else in the business you can talk to? I'm still trying to figure out where this girl came from."

"I've been wondering the same thing." Elena paused for a beat. "I saw her picture on the internet. Let me make some calls, and I'll get back to you, okay?"

After we hung up, I went and found Noah. We fished down on the dock for a few hours—rather, he fished while I watched and played with Boss. Bryce texted me after lunch: *Pack your bags, babe. We're leaving for Boston tonight.*

Great! I texted back. He'd only been crazy with work for a few days, but I was more than ready to be reunited with him. The short plane ride was an opportunity to be close, even if he had to tackle his emails.

Plus, he'd mentioned that shower bench...

I quickly put down my phone. "Noah! Will you be okay if I go to Boston with Bryce for the next few nights? He needs to visit the company headquarters."

Noah cast his line out again. "You're kidding, right? I'm so happy here. Chef's making me homemade pizza tonight. Dale challenged me to a video game tournament, and Lilly said she'd bring her puppy out to play with Boss later. You guys can go to Timbuktu for all I care!"

"Gee, thanks." But my feelings weren't really hurt. How could I compete with puppies and X-box?

I glimpsed a flash of blond in my peripheral vision—Colby and Tate were walking down the path from the guesthouse. They appeared to be deep in conversation. Colby scratched his head as he watched Tate, who was talking with an animated expression on her face. They stopped, and he pulled her in for an embrace. After a moment, they broke apart. Colby headed for the house; Tate made a phone call.

My phone rang. I answered it and looked up.

From the path, Tate stared directly at me. Another unpleasant expression marred her pretty face. "Can you come here? We need to talk."

We need to talk. Were there ever four worse words than that? They lodged in my stomach, forming a pit of dread.

"Sure."

I hung up the phone and headed toward her, even though I'd never been less sure in my life.

due diligence

CHLOE

TATE WORE an expensive designer-brand fleece jacket, short hiking shorts, and trail shoes. She was easing into the look of a wealthy Maine socialite, her thick, blond hair, toned figure, and clear skin rounding out the picture.

"I need to talk to you," she said. "In private."

"Okay..." I glanced around the grounds; there was no one in sight. "We should be good."

"Both Olivia Jensen and Daphne are up my ass—not to mention that creepy maid Hazel. I don't trust any of them. Let's go for a walk." Tate headed back down the path without waiting for me. I scrambled to keep up with her.

"How's everything going?" I asked.

She shrugged. "It could be better."

"What's wrong?"

She glanced at me, narrowing her eyes. "The person who hired me isn't happy right now. I might lose the job."

"I'm surprised by that. Colby seems very taken with you."

Her brow furrowed. "You think?"

"This is the first time you've been apart in days," I said. "Every time I see you together, he has his arm around you."

"That's true..." She scowled and twisted a lock of her hair around her finger. "But my client doesn't care about that as much as what's happening with *you*. She says I'm not doing enough."

She. Tate's client was a woman. The pit of dread in my stomach got heavier as my brain started running calculations in the background. "*She?*" I blinked at Tate. "You're client is a she?"

Tate's nostrils flared. "I didn't say that. Anyway, it doesn't matter."

"What exactly does she want you to do?"

"Make your life a living hell. Embarrass you. Remind you that you're nothing and that you could lose your spot at any moment. She's—ugh, *they've*—been pissed at me ever since that party." Her scowl deepened. "But I had to keep Colby happy, and you and Bryce were stuck to each other like glue, making goo-goo eyes all night..."

She groaned. "Olivia Jensen's up my ass. She's watching my every move! I can't really do anything except stay on the island and have sex with Colby. You're always with your brother or Daphne, just talking and hanging out. What does she want me to *do*, anyway? Get you so drunk you pass out, so I can take naked pictures of you and post them on the internet?"

"Sorry Tate, I don't drink."

"I freaking know it! This is impossible. I knew it was too good to be true, all the money she promised me..." She cursed under her breath. "The thing is, I like it here. Colby's a nice guy. He's good to me. I never had a guy be good to me before."

I sighed, thinking of my father. "I understand. Colby *is* a nice guy."

"Right? Who the fuck knew they existed? And this" —Tate gestured to the island—"this is the nicest place I've ever been in my life. I don't want to go back to my crappy apartment. One of my roommates does drugs and has a *weasel*. The apartment *reeks*, and all sorts of randoms are always passed out in the living room. But it was all I could afford, you know? A few weeks before I found that place, I was living on the streets..."

Tate shuddered. "I never finished high school. I don't have a family. I had a boyfriend who screwed me and took all my money—that's why I started working as an escort. I have *nothing*, Chloe. *Nothing*. I don't want to get fired! I don't want to go back to either the druggies and the weasel or the streets. I don't want to be an escort anymore. You, of all people, must understand."

My heart twisted. "Of course I understand." I'd only ever had one job—marrying Bryce—but my experience on the dating app SugarFinder and dealing with AccommoDating had opened my eyes to a realm of dark possibilities I'd never known about. I didn't blame Tate one bit for not wanting to go back. Who the hell would?

"So, can you help me?" Tate asked.

"I don't know *how* to help you. But I can tell you that my marriage is real. I love Bryce. Maybe there's a chance for you and Colby...?"

She shook her head. "That's not ever going to happen for me."

"I understand—I felt the same way. But it did work out."

Tate's brow furrowed, a cloudy expression descending over her features. "Things don't work out for girls like me. I'm not holding my breath for you, either."

"Gee, thanks."

She shrugged. "I'm just telling you the truth. Who else around here's going to do that?"

My phone buzzed with a text, and I glanced at it: it was from an unknown number, which was Gene Windsor's calling card of private-message death. "I have to go. I don't feel like we really accomplished anything—"

"Hold on—I still need to do something bad to you." Tate inspected me. "Unless you have some sort of other idea?"

"I don't see myself volunteering to get drunk, naked, and posing for social media anytime soon. Sorry." I felt my anxiety mounting—I needed to deal with Gene's message, but I also needed to deal with whomever it was that hired Tate. My enemies were mounting their attacks against me. Gene Windsor, Mimi Jones, Felicia Jones, probably my freaking step-monster, Lydia...

But Gene was already busy blackmailing me, and Lydia couldn't afford a high-end escort. That left Mimi and Felicia Jones.

Something clicked inside me. *I know where you came from and all about your little arrangement.* Mimi Jones's slurred words from the party came back to me, landing with a *thud* in my stomach right alongside the pit of dread. *Come near my daughter again, I'll expose you for the whore you are.*

Tate's employer was a she, and I knew exactly who it was. *Fuck!*

"Why don't you just lie to her?" I blurted out, not even knowing where the thought was coming from. "Tell her Bryce and I got into a huge fight the other night after the party because I'm so jealous of Felicia, I can't see straight. Say that he was all over me because we were in public, but he's been very hands-off at home."

A plan started forming in my mind. "Make her think I'm on the outs with Bryce and that our relationship is an act because he needs good press. Tell her you're getting close to me. Tell her I'm falling apart. Promise you'll keep feeding her information."

Tate arched an eyebrow. "That... That might work."

"It'll at least buy you some time." I shrugged, still not knowing where the inspiration had come from. Maybe being blackmailed by so many people had given me some ideas!

"By the way, Mimi Jones is pretty scary. If she fires you, it might be the best thing that ever happened to you." I turned on my heel and hustled back toward the house, all the better to listen to Gene's latest message in private.

Tate threw up her hands. "Where are you going?"

"I have a meeting. Keep me posted on Mimi!"

"I never said it was her!" Tate hollered, but I didn't answer.

I didn't need to. We both knew the truth.

As soon as I got inside, I ducked into one of the bathrooms and locked the door behind me.

Once again, Attorney Finley appeared on my screen.

"My client was unhappy with the amount of detail you provided to our point of contact this morning," she said. "Moving forward, we will be having these exchanges directly. I'm sending you a secure link to a form—please upload more specific information regarding this matter and then hit 'submit.'"

She blinked at the screen. "And Mrs. Windsor, please be advised that my client is frustrated with you. So you best be more diligent. Good day."

The screen went dark, and I shivered.

The link popped up and I clicked on it. The subject line read *Personal Information,* and then there was space to write in the details.

I took a deep breath, weighing my options.

Gene was against me, but he wanted to use me to maintain control over his family.

Mimi was against me, and she wanted to humiliate me, infiltrate the family, and take revenge against the Windsors.

They were both bad. But who was worse? That was a question I couldn't answer just yet.

I needed to tell the truth, but how much of it? I wanted to ensure my actions didn't make it worse for anyone—like my brother, my husband, and myself. Even though she'd threatened me, I didn't want to make it any worse for Tate, either.

I started writing.

I don't know much about Tate except that she didn't just bump into Colby by accident. Someone hired her. Someone is paying her to be here, to watch the family.

I took another deep breath.

I believe it was Mimi Jones.

Then: *I believe we can use this to our advantage.*

I hit submit and wondered, not for the first time, just what the hell I'd gotten myself into.

allegiances

CHLOE

DAPHNE ACCOSTED me before we left for the Bar Harbor airport. "What do you mean you're leaving again?"

"It's just for the weekend," I explained. "Bryce needs to be down at headquarters, and he wanted me to go with him. It'll look good for me to support him as he takes on a more public role. At least, that's what Olivia Jensen said."

The truth was, I couldn't care less about the PR angle—I just wanted to be with my husband! Not to mention to get a break from the pit of vipers that surrounded me on MDI.

She put her hands on her hips. "Are you sure that's what you should be doing right now? Aren't you supposed to be, I don't know, minding your business around here? Keeping an eye on things—like Tate?"

"Tate's a person, not a thing."

"Are you sure about that?" Daphne arched her eyebrow. "And did you find out anything else about her?"

"What do you mean?"

Daphne shrugged. "Nothing. Just curious."

But it didn't seem like nothing. Something about how she acted reminded me of the other night at the Nguyen's party...

"Oh boy—here comes Bryce. I better move over. You're supposed to be next to him all night, right?" Daphne winked at me and hustled away.

"Right." Gene Windsor had been crystal-clear that I was to stand by my husband and stay out of trouble all night.

But...how the hell did Daphne know about that?

I considered Daphne a friend. Still, that didn't mean I could blindly trust her. She was as motivated by money and power as anyone else who surrounded me at the moment.

I decided to switch gears. "Daphne... How is everything with you and Gene? Are you able to talk to him regularly?"

She shrugged. "Not exactly, because of the prison's restrictions. But we've been in contact."

"So, are you planning on staying together?"

Daphne turned and stared at her enormous mansion. "I guess it all depends."

"On what?"

She sighed. "On a lot of things."

"Is it about the money?" I guessed.

"Isn't it always?" She sighed again. "I don't know about you, but I'm never going back to 'normal' life. I can't. So I'm just hanging on here and seeing what needs to be done. You never know with my husband—you just never know what he's going to ask for."

True, Daphne. Very true.

I squeezed her arm. "I hope Michael Jones comes through for you with a big settlement offer. Ten million dollars is a lot of money, Daphne. You could do whatever you wanted if you got that—you and the baby would both be taken care of."

"I know, but... Ten million doesn't really seem like enough when you can have ten *billion*, you know?" She kept staring at the house. "Gene makes you work for it, though. It's not easy being in this family."

I stood by her side, staring at the enormous ocean-front mansion. "You're right about that."

As expected, Bryce had a ton of emails to catch up on during the short plane ride to Boston. I didn't mind at all. I sat happily by his side, nestled against his big body.

Heaven. If heaven could be a place on earth, this was it: right by my husband's side.

"You're being quiet," he said as we landed. "But I guess that's because I've been on my laptop non-stop. Sorry about that. And unfortunately, I have to go into the office for a few hours tonight. The government informed our legal team that they're about to announce a pre-trial date. Jury selection will begin sooner than we thought, and we have to be prepared for how this will impact our stock valuation."

I squeezed his hand. "That sounds like a lot. How is the board? How does everyone feel about all this?"

He blew out a deep breath. "Everything's up in the air right now. I'm personally prepared for the fact that my father's probably going to be convicted and that we'll be forced to move forward from that. But Regina Hernandez and some of the others aren't so sure. They want a plan in place in case that *doesn't* happen."

"You mean if he isn't convicted?"

Bryce nodded. "They aren't sure that they want him to come back. They might want me to stay on as CEO."

"Wow." I blinked at him. "That's a *huge* deal. How do you feel about it?"

He was quiet for a moment as our bags were loaded into a sleek black SUV. Once we climbed inside and the driver sped toward Beacon Hill, he said, "It's what I've always wanted. And now that my father went and did this, I feel like I have the exact reason for taking over that I've been looking for. My father is greedy and only wants what's best for himself—always. Now everyone knows it."

Bryce held my hand as he stared out the window. The Boston skyline was streaked with pink, the city lights just beginning to wink out from the windows. "I believe we can serve a higher purpose with our company, and I'd like to grow it into something that our family can be proud of. We'll still make tons of money, but there are lots of opportunities to innovate and do good things in the world. My father has never capitalized on that. He's too afraid of risking what he has. His wealth has always been the most important thing to him. I can't blame him for that. But I grew up different than he did—I've *always* had it all, and I realize I don't need more to feel secure."

"Your dad didn't grow up with much?" I asked.

He shrugged. "His family had money, just not the kind of money he has now. I think he always had a chip on his shoulder, but I don't know why. He's never been one to talk about his childhood or his feelings. Although I think he could do that with my mom. I told you, he's never been the same since she died."

"That's too bad." But it was hard to muster up much sympathy for the man who was blackmailing me.

"There's nothing I can do about it. I need to focus on the present and our company. The truth is, I have— *we* have—everything we need for our family and our family's future. The time to move forward with Windsor Enterprises is now. And I want to do it. I don't know what my father will do when he hears about this. He'll view it as a coup."

My heart sank. "You're right. Is someone telling him what's going on?" Knowing Gene Windsor, he had spies on the board who were actively reporting to him.

"Board members are in touch with him, yes. And I'm sure that he has eyes and ears watching me."

Ugh. I was Gene's eyes and ears, too. At least he hadn't asked me anything about my husband. *Yet.*

"But people are scared right now," Bryce continued. "They don't know if he's ever going to come back and be in charge. It's a tricky time for allegiances, you know what I mean?"

I watched the darkening sky and held onto my husband for dear life. "I sure do, Bryce. I sure do."

"We just need to keep our heads down," he said. "You stay close. I'll keep trying to be the voice of reason with the board. It'll all work out."

"I hope so." But I felt sick as I imagined Gene Windsor hearing about the change in circumstances. What would he do if he knew the board was considering taking such an extreme action? I shivered and shoved the question away—I didn't want to know the answer. But deep down, I knew that he would be furious, and a furious Gene Windsor was a scary thought.

Bryce had the driver drop me off at the townhouse in Beacon Hill. He kissed me goodbye as one of his employees brought our bags in. "The local staff already opened the house up and stocked everything," he told me. "I've dismissed everyone except for security. You should have plenty of privacy, but I'll know you're safe."

He kissed the top of my head. "Feel free to go to bed, but I might wake you up when I get home."

I grinned up at him. "Sounds good, Mr. Windsor."

"I love you, Mrs. Windsor. I'll see you later." With another kiss, my handsome husband ducked back inside the SUV. I watched as it pulled down the street, feeling bereft.

What would happen if the board voted him in as full-term CEO?

Bryce would be happy about it. More importantly, he would be *good* at it. I didn't know much about the company, but I knew *that*. He was a strong man who would make decent choices. He would steer Windsor Enterprises into new territory and would use his position and power in a way that his father never had.

He was born for the role.

But would his own father stand in the way of his destiny?

I had every reason to fear that he would.

discovery

CHLOE

THEN I TURNED to face his spectacular Boston home and felt overwhelmed. It was a white townhouse stretching four-stories high. Trees peeped over the top—there must be some magnificent roof deck up there. A marble staircase led to the entrance, a massive, ornate door surrounded by an intricate black-metal design. As I climbed the stairs, I felt like Dorothy landing in Oz, completely out of my freaking element.

I'd grown up in Boston, but this was *not* the Boston that I knew.

"Mrs. Windsor." The employee who'd brought my luggage in held the door open for me. "There are several of us on duty, but we'll stay out of your way. Please just use one of the intercoms in the house if you need us." He disappeared down a hall, leaving me alone in the entryway, which opened directly to the living room.

It was a good thing he left—I didn't have to be self-conscious about gaping.

The home was immaculate, with white walls, gleaming hardwood floors, and clean New England style. A fire roared in the fireplace. The white couches and modern lighting contrasted with the classic feel of the house, giving it a balanced, fresh feeling. I picked my way through the gorgeous room, careful not to knock into anything, and looked out the wall of rear-facing windows. The Charles River was in plain view, the after-work crowd running and biking along it.

People were out there, living their lives like any other day. But I felt like my world was falling apart. There was no one I could trust anymore, not even myself. I could trust Bryce, of course, but he didn't know what I was going through. And really, it wasn't safe for me to be close to him. Both Gene Windsor and Mimi Jones were after me. What was I supposed to do?

My phone buzzed with a text from Olivia Jensen. *Please send pics of you in the Boston house. People will love a sneak peek inside. Get dressed up and put on makeup!*

I longed to text back that she was clueless. That

what she was asking me to do was so beside the point, it was laughable.

Sure thing, I texted back instead. At least it would give me something to do!

I wandered upstairs to the enormous primary suite. It also looked out on the Charles and had spectacular views of the Boston skyline. I sat on the bed and ran my hands down the pristine, cool comforter, imagining sleeping next to Bryce in the vast bed that night. I couldn't wait for him to come home from the office, to be reunited with him...

I wandered to the closet. I was unsurprised to find an entire wardrobe in exactly my size. There were a ton of dresses, blouses, skirts, and shoes, all completely brand-new and designer. I wondered if Midge had shopped for all of this and had it sent down or if Bryce had other employees who did such things. It was crazy to think someone had bought all these clothes for *me*. I ran my hand down the rack, reveling in the feel of the silky shirts and luxurious-feeling fabrics.

I checked the time—Bryce wouldn't be home for hours.

I decided to put everything else aside and have some fun for once. I went to the bureau and selected some gorgeous lace lingerie from La Perla. I'd googled the brand after Midge insisted that I wear it. The thongs sold for three hundred dollars a pop! I slid on a pair of red ones and found a matching bra. Never in my dreams did I expect to end up wearing high-end lingerie in a multi-million-dollar home. I couldn't believe I was in Beacon Hill, waiting for my billionaire husband to come home from work.

I was feeling myself in the red lingerie—wearing a thousand dollars worth of red lace could do that to a girl! I stalked to the gorgeous white-tiled bathroom. I found the stockpile of expensive makeup and sat down at the expertly lit mirror. I was no Midge, but I did the best I could, grooming my brows, applying light foundation, putting on mascara and a little lip gloss. I returned to the bedroom and whipped out my phone when I was done. I laid back on the bed and made kissy faces at the camera, making sure a glimpse of the red bralette was visible.

Thinking of you, I texted Bryce.

He wrote back immediately. *Are you fucking kidding me? I'M STUCK IN A BOARD MEETING—FML!* He included a crying with laughter emoji.

I'll be waiting for you, I wrote back.

Don't you dare take that off, he wrote back. *I'll be home as soon as I can.*

Sighing, I decided to get dressed and take the pictures that Olivia had asked for. First, I put on a proper navy sheath and took selfies by the fireplace. Next, I changed into a silk blouse, a black skirt, and knee-high suede boots. I posed in the gorgeous kitchen, smiling, acting like I had some actual business wearing insanely expensive clothes and grinning in a billion-aire's kitchen. I changed again, this time into a formal red gown that swept the floor because...why the hell not? I stood by the windows, ensuring the glittering skyline was visible in the background.

I sent the files to Olivia, then padded to the kitchen for a glass of water.

As soon as I had a sip, something felt wrong. My stomach twisted.

I ran into the downstairs powder room—no small feat in the gown—and threw up, waves of nausea rippling through me. I slumped on the cool tile floor, waiting for the next round. But as suddenly as the sick feeling had come, it was gone. Weird!

I went upstairs and changed out of the dress, feeling off-kilter and more than a little silly about the pictures I'd taken. But Olivia texted me back: *These are great. Nice work!* At least I'd accomplished something that day.

I went to the bathroom and brushed my teeth. As soon as I tasted the minty toothpaste, it happened again: I threw up suddenly and definitively, even though there wasn't much in my stomach.

But as soon as I was finished, I felt fine again. Fine, as in, not even a little sick. *I must have some weird sort of bug!*

I texted Midge, curious to know if anyone else at the house was feeling ill.

No hon, we are all fine. Three dots appeared, then disappeared, then appeared again.

When was the last time you had your period?

I stared at the screen. I didn't blink. I didn't breathe.

And then I ran into the bathroom and threw up again.

I waited up for Bryce, but just as it was about to turn midnight, I gave up and turned off my light.

Then my phone beeped.

I lunged for it, hoping it was my husband, but instead, it was yet another link to a secure message from Gene Windsor.

Attorney Finley once again blinked at the screen. Did she have nothing better to do than play messenger for her billionaire client? Probably not...

"Mrs. Windsor, we have a situation. My client has learned that the board is considering electing Bryce Windsor as full-fledged CEO, essentially removing my client from his duties. The vote could happen as early as Monday. We will need you to get as much information from your husband as possible regarding the particulars and his plans with respect to this appointment."

The attorney took a deep breath. "My client wants you to understand that this can't be allowed to happen. We'll give you further instructions as more details emerge. Please submit the secure form once you've had a chance to speak with your husband. Do not let more than twenty-four hours elapse before you submit it. Good evening, Mrs. Windsor."

But as I put down the phone, I knew there was nothing good about it. Nothing at all.

doubt

BRYCE

I HAD A GODDAMNED erection ever since Chloe sent me that text. How was I supposed to concentrate on the board meeting?

But it was crucial that I pay attention. Regina Hernandez was talking about making me the official CEO of Windsor Enterprises. I was now the interim, but the board was losing confidence in my father. They seemed just as concerned that he would get out of jail as they were about him being convicted. There was a lot of loyalty to my father, but the times were changing. Even the board members who had served under Gene the longest were talking about changing the company's direction.

My father had shaken the foundation of Windsor Enterprises. Those of us who were left had a new perspective. They said they wanted *me* to lead.

This was my moment.

When my father heard that they planned to take it to a vote, he was going to lose his mind. I was a little afraid, actually. What would he do to try to retain control of his empire?

The meeting lasted until the early hours of the morning. I found Chloe fast asleep when I got to the townhouse after two a.m. Good girl that she was, she still had on that red lace bra. I peeked under the covers and caught sight of the matching thong. My erection raged, but I couldn't bring myself to wake her up. She looked so peaceful. I slid into bed beside her, and she murmured as she snuggled up against my chest.

This did nothing to ease my raging hard-on, but I ignored it. I hadn't slept well in days, and damn if the bed didn't feel great. It felt even better because Chloe was here.

I held her close, thinking about how much my life had changed since I'd met her. I'd spent many nights alone in Boston. Sometimes I had women at the house, but they never slept over, and I never had them in my bedroom. I wanted no one close to me, especially after what happened with Felicia. Sex was a need, but there was no intimacy. They came, I came, and they went.

Lying there with my wife in my arms, I could see that my life had been pretty empty.

Everything was different now. I was on the cusp of actually taking power at Windsor Enterprises. There was a real chance my father would spend the rest of his life in jail. Even if he was cleared of the charges, the board wanted me to lead. I could finally make a difference.

Not only that, but I was married to the woman of my dreams. I hadn't known I needed Chloe—I thought I was fine on my own. But once I'd opened my heart to her, she'd shown me just how incredible my life could be.

Even though things had been difficult, I couldn't underestimate the happiness my marriage had brought me. Feeling secure in my relationship brought my confidence to a new level. My father had been wrong about so many things, but perhaps he was right about that: marriage made you a man.

Chloe's brow furrowed in sleep, like maybe she was having a bad dream. "It's okay, babe. I've got you," I whispered and held her close.

We fell asleep like that, wrapped in each other's arms.

I woke up before her. I glanced at the clock: five a.m. I would have to go to the office again soon.

But first, I was going to wake Chloe up. I *needed* her.

"Babe." I nuzzled my face against hers, and she shivered against me. "I have to get up for work in a minute."

"No, don't." She buried her face against my chest and stretched out against me. I was already rock-hard against her. She knew it, too—she wriggled against me, her belly pressing against the tip of my cock. She kissed my chest, trailing up higher to my neck, then kissed my jawline.

She pulled back and squinted up at me. "Good morning, Handsome."

"Good morning, Gorgeous. Do you have a minute for me before I have to go?"

She nodded, grinning, and my heart did a somersault. To me, Chloe was the most beautiful girl in the world. When she smiled at me, it was like the sun coming out.

She pressed herself against my cock again, and the familiar, insistent heat built up between us.

"We don't have that long, unfortunately. But I'll get out early tonight, so I can treat my wife right."

Her pupils dilated as she looked up at me expectantly.

"I told you about that shower bench. I intend to use it, but that's for later, babe." I kissed her neck, and she arched against me, her smooth, cool skin making mine ignite with sparks.

I unclasped her bra, freeing her spectacular breasts, and greedily palmed them. Her nipples hardened, and I pinched them, taking one in my mouth as we writhed against each other.

Chloe raked her hands over my chest, palming the muscles. She ran her hands down my pectoral muscles worshipfully, and it made me hard, so hard, as did seeing her naked tits bounce beneath me. I rolled on top of her, skimming my hand down her sides and in between her legs. I could feel the thin lace of the thong already soaking wet. I ripped it off and spread her legs apart, her sex glistening below me.

"You're already wet for me."

"Of course I am, Bryce. I was home all night waiting for you, alone in this bed." She ran her hands down her own body to her sex, mesmerizing me. "I was thinking about you all night."

My breathing became ragged as her fingers trailed down to her sex. She moaned as she touched herself. My cock was so hard it was about to burst.

"What were you thinking?"

"About being with you. Like this." She ran her fingers down herself one more time and then moved to me, swirling the wetness at my tip.

Then she started to milk me. "I was thinking about doing this."

"Oh fuck." Her grip tightened and it felt so, so good. I kissed her again, my cock searing fiercely between us. "Babe. I need a time out with that." I had to stop her before she made me come!

She reluctantly released me, and I took a steadying breath. *Not yet.* My lips trailed down her neck, over her breasts, along her belly to her sex. Fuck, she tasted so good. I ran my tongue along her slit and she cried out, making me crazy.

I was going to bring her to the edge and leave her there. I wanted to make her lose control, to give herself to me, to show her that I was the only one who could *ever* give her what she wanted.

She threw her arms around me, and hot pride bloomed inside my chest. *Mine. Mine. MINE.* Something about the fact that I'd been Chloe's first, that I'd claimed her, unleashed a primal instinct in me. I wanted to give her everything. I wanted to give her all of me and take all of *her.* I was her only lover, and she was mine forever.

My tongue lashed against her clit, her muscles spasming. Chloe arched her back as I sucked her hard, increasing the pressure with my tongue. I put two fingers inside her, penetrating her as my tongue massaged her sex.

"Bryce—oh *fuck!*" She came, hard, shattering around my fingers. Her body was still bucking against me as I notched myself at her entrance. Her tight little body was still spasming as I entered her. Slowly at first, until I'd entered her fully.

"Bryce, oh my God—"

Her name on my lips pushed me over the edge—I began fucking her *hard. Yes. Fuck, yes.* Her pussy spasmed around me, gripping me, making my world go white. She grazed her nails down my back, but I grabbed both her hands and pinned them over her head. I drove hard, deep; Chloe met me stroke for stroke, grinding herself against my shaft. *Holy fuck.* The pressure built, the intensity built, as we both drove for home. Her body quivered—she was on the edge, and I was right there with her. I increased my thrusts, ass pumping as she shattered beneath me again.

The orgasm built inside me, eclipsing everything. "Oh, oh *fuck!*" My balls tightened, and I came hard, my orgasm chasing hers. I shot myself inside her, emptying myself, our bodies inexorably becoming one. She cried out again as the aftershocks of her orgasm mingled with mine. Tears streamed down her face.

"Babe, hey, it's okay." I cradled her in my arms as she started to cry. "What's the matter?"

"N-Nothing." But she clung to my chest as the tears fell. "That was just intense."

I laughed. "It was for me, too. Pass the tissues," I joked.

But I stopped laughing as we pulled apart and saw the puffiness surrounding Chloe's eyes. She'd looked peaceful as she'd slept, but now she seemed uneasy.

"What's the matter?" I asked more seriously.

She wiped her eyes, then gazed up at me. "Nothing. I just missed you. Is everything okay at the office?"

"Everything's great." I kissed the top of her head and hugged her to me. "They're talking about doing the vote on Monday. I feel good about it, Chloe. I think everything's working out the way it should."

"What about your Dad?" Her voice came out muffled against my chest.

I shrugged. "He'll be fine. Even if he's not fine, he'll be fine. You know?"

She nodded against my chest but didn't say another word.

Unfortunately, I couldn't stay with her—I had an

early meeting. Kissing the top of her head again, I headed for the shower.

But as I left my wife in the bed where we'd just made love, I had a sinking feeling. There was a reason Chloe was crying, and it wasn't just because of an orgasm. It couldn't be.

So... What was my wife hiding from me?

tightrope

CHLOE

AFTER BRYCE LEFT for the office, I grabbed my phone. Gene Windsor's attorney had sent me another secure link.

Both Gene Windsor and his attorney could go die in a hole, for all I cared.

I ignored the link and instead went to my calendar. When the heck *did* I get my last period? I kept zero record of it, of course. Elena had encouraged me to download some sort of app to track it, but I'd blithely ignored her. I'd *also* blithely ignored that I wasn't on birth control, and Bryce and I had had sex about a zillion times.

I shivered, remembering our encounter from that morning. He'd made me come so hard, I'd seen stars. And then I'd started crying because I was so scared about his father, what his father would ask of me...

The fact that I might be pregnant just complicated everything further. What if Gene forced me to leave Bryce again? What the hell was I going to do then?

I put down my phone, climbed out of bed, and started pacing. I couldn't let my mask slip in front of my husband again. If I betrayed Gene, he would hurt Bryce —not to mention my brother. I felt like I was walking a tightrope, and everyone's existence depended on my performance. The thing was, I didn't have very good balance. And I'd never had much of a game face.

I didn't know what to do or where to turn.

There was no one I could trust.

It was too early to call Dale and check in on my brother, but I had to do something. I hustled to the shower and washed my hair. As I stood under the hot water, I ran my hands over my stomach. Was it possible that I was pregnant?

What would Bryce think?

I could picture him being excited, picking out baby names, and bragging to his brothers. *Stop it, Chloe.*

Every time I pictured a happy future with Bryce, I

had to make myself stop. Gene Windsor wasn't going to let that happen. If I let myself hope, it would be much worse when my dreams crashed and burned.

After getting dressed in a simple black dress that was still ridiculously fancy for everyday wear, I headed downstairs. Worried that my nausea would return, I bypassed the kitchen and went to the front door.

"Mrs. Windsor?" One of Bryce's besuited men appeared out of nowhere. "Are we going out?"

"Um... I was just going to run to the drugstore. I wasn't feeling well."

"Can I go pick something up for you?" he asked.

"I'd like to go if that's okay. I'm not sure what I need."

"I'll just go with you." He wasn't taking no for an answer. "I'll follow behind and give you plenty of privacy, I promise."

"Thanks," I said weakly. But who the hell actually had privacy in a situation like this?

My thoughts swirled as I headed down the street, the early morning air fresh and clean. Beacon Hill was spectacular, with gorgeous, immaculately maintained townhouses lining the streets and gardens brimming with bursting late-summer flowers. I inhaled deeply, hoping the fresh air could cleanse my circling, anxious thoughts.

Gene wanted me to tell him everything about what the board was planning and how Bryce felt about it. My inclination was to act clueless, but was that safe? Gene already knew that the board was considering voting on Bryce's position. If he was aware of that, what else did he know? The problem was that I sucked at lying. Not only that, I didn't know where his information began and where it ended. What would happen if I mischaracterized or omitted something and Gene realized it? Would I be jeopardizing my brother's already precarious position? What about Bryce? Was I helping him or hurting him by doing what Gene asked?

A drugstore was on the corner and I ducked into it, hoping to lose my security-guard friend. But he was right behind me. He kept close as I browsed the pain reliever section, pretending to compare brands of ibuprofen.

Finally, I had an idea. "Hey." Now I was the one who magically appeared at *his* side. "I need to go to this aisle." I pointed to the sign that said *Feminine Care*. He gave me a thumbs-up and followed me to the aisle, but he didn't venture down into the land of maxi pads and tampons, God bless him.

I went to work quickly. I grabbed several large boxes of feminine supplies and vitamins and quickly shoved three pregnancy tests between my wares. Then I hustled to the checkout counter, blocking my purchases with my body and the enormous designer handbag I'd grabbed from the closet. Once everything was paid for, I slid the tests into my tote and carried everything else out in the plastic shopping bag.

The guard didn't say a word and didn't offer to carry my bagful of feminine-care products. *Score.* Once we were back at the house, I unpacked everything and hid the extra tests in one of my new Stuart Weitzman over-the-knee suede boots.

I clasped the other test and headed for the bathroom, but the intercom intercepted me.

"Mrs. Windsor?" The guard sounded slightly panicked. 'There's someone here to see you."

I stopped dead in my tracks. "Who is it?"

"She said she's your stepmother."

"It's me, Lydia!" She hollered. "Get your ass down here, this idiot's trying to throw me out! I'm going to sue him and everyone else if he doesn't shut his yap and get out of my way!"

"Hold on, I'll be right down!" *Fuck!* I quickly hid the test under the sink and ran downstairs. Lydia had a short fuse. I had no doubt she would try to shut the guard's yap or die trying. I rushed to the bottom of the stairs and found two of the guards facing off with my step-monster. The men were stone-faced, but Lydia's cheeks were flushed, her hands curled into fists. Her orange-y hair was slicked back into a bun, and her shorts revealed her newest tattoo, the giant face of a lion.

"Hey guys—that's my stepmother. She's fine." 'Fine' wasn't an accurate description, but I still waved them away.

I motioned for Lydia to follow me into the living room. Once we were alone, I whirled on her. "What the hell are you doing here?" I hissed.

"Checking on my one-and-only step-daughter." Her voice was too loud. Everything about her was too much; I had to squint at her to soften my view of her orangey-blond hair and smoker's lines. "You haven't been in touch, Chloe. I thought we had a deal."

I shook my head. "I don't know what you're talking about. I thought you and Dad were happy with the money we gave you. Dad signed the agreement—I thought we were done with it."

"Well, turns out we're not quite done just yet." She smiled, revealing newly whitened teeth. "I need more from you and your husband."

"Lydia." I shook my head. "We've already given you a ton of money. There isn't any more."

"Ha!" Her laughter quickly turned to a phlegmy cough. "How can you say that with a straight face? Look at this place! I saw on one of those real-estate apps that it's worth twenty million bucks—and this is just one of your husband's houses!"

I took a deep breath. My stepmother's greed knew no bounds. First came the tattoo, then the whitened teeth. Next was probably the facelift and the condo, not to mention a lifetime supply of cigarettes and liquor. Who the hell knew what else she wanted?

"I have to tell you, it took some time for me and your father to figure it out. We thought the older guy would be the biggest payout. But it turns out there's *way* more money to be made than just that old cocksucker. He *is* a whiny little bitch, isn't he?"

I refused to agree with her. But deep down, I knew she was right: Gene Windsor really was a little bitch.

"What's happening with him? How much money did he give you?"

She snorted. "He was all talk at first—real promising. But then he's only coughed up half-a-mill, not really enough to make it worthwhile for us to keep our mouths shut about you."

"Between that and the money we've given you, you're *rich*. You should be happy—"

"Don't tell me what I should be!" She flopped down onto the nearest couch and whipped out a pack of cigarettes. Lydia lit up without asking permission, exhaling a dirty cloud above her head. The smoke was woefully out of place in the pristine living room, but then again, so was Lydia. "I'm the one telling *you*. You should listen, not talk."

She took another deep drag off her cigarette and blew out a toxic cloud. My step-monster was taking her time, enjoying herself.

That made one of us.

I sank down onto a nearby chair. "What do you want, Lydia?"

"We want more. Your father and I deserve *more*. We took you and your brother in when your mom died, even though we didn't have the space, and you were always ungrateful. But we did our best." Lydia straightened her shoulders defiantly.

"Now you're all rich and fancy," she continued, "and you think your shit doesn't stink. But it does, let me tell you. And plenty of people out there think it stinks, too. So you're going to pay up. Otherwise, I'll do what these rich people are asking me to."

"What are they asking you to do?"

"Well, that depends." She exhaled another cloud of smoke, and I wished a lightning bolt would shoot out of it and crack her straight in the head. But alas, she just kept talking. "Mr. Windsor wanted us to sit tight and hold off on filing anything for your brother and not go to the press. But this other lady wants us to go public about your background, do interviews, and all sorts of stuff. And she'd been paying pretty good. But I figured that since you were married to the richest dude of them all—and he's seemed pretty dead-set against us talking —he might want to outbid her. After all, it's his pretty little wife she's talking about."

She flicked some ash onto the floor. "She's saying you're a hooker, can you believe it? And here you are, sitting all high and mighty in that dress. Like I said, Chlo, your shit absolutely stinks. Doesn't matter if you're spraying Chanel perfume all over it. A hooker is a hooker. Your father couldn't believe *that* one, but I told him it's always the quiet ones you gotta watch out for!" She laugh-coughed again, thoroughly amused by herself.

"Who is the woman who's paying you?" But I already knew.

"Some rich cunt from Maine. You beat up her daughter." Lydia's features twisted. "Mimi something-or-other?"

I nodded. "Mimi Jones. You're right that she's rich— but you're also right that we're richer."

"Good." Lydia took another big drag. "I'm glad to hear you say that, Chlo. I'm sure that handsome husband of yours doesn't want the world to know he married a skank."

The fact that Lydia was calling me a skank was indeed the icing on the fucking cake. "How much do you want, Lydia?"

She sat back, smiling. "A lot. I want a lot."

games people play

CHLOE

IT WAS all fun and games until the blackmail started.

Lydia had asked me for *five million dollars*. And I said *yes*. Gene had told her he was good for up to a million. She felt that Mimi Jones had lowballed her at seven-hundred-and-fifty thousand.

I needed to be the most generous so that I bought her loyalty. It definitely wasn't worth five million, but it was worth *something*. I hoped.

No matter who ended up paying what, Lydia and my father were moving up a few tax brackets.

As to how she'd gotten our Beacon Hill address, she said Mimi Jones had texted it to her. "She wanted me to call WMUR and bring them with me to surprise you,"

Lydia said. "But I figured your husband might pay more, so I wanted to talk first."

"You were right." She would never stop extorting us; I might as well accept that and pray they didn't blow through all the money at once at another casino.

I didn't know how Bryce was going to react to more blackmail. But at the moment, I had to make Lydia happy so she would leave us alone.

I sat alone for hours, reeling after Lydia had left. I was too upset to text Bryce and tell him what had happened. There were too many red flags to count, but this seemed a clear indication that Mimi Jones was completely out to get me. Tate wasn't her only weapon.

Fuck! Like I needed more trouble!

And I still needed to deal with uploading Gene's stupid form. What did he want from me, anyway? To sell my husband out? Deep down, I feared that was *exactly* what he wanted...

My last face-to-face conversation with him echoed inside my head.

"The way I see it, I'm still saving my company. I have a new perspective on things. Like I said, desperation makes things very clear. I know what I want now. I want my company to go on the way it was intended. I want Bryce to run things the way he's supposed to...

If Bryce was about to be voted in as full CEO, Gene

wouldn't feel his son was running the company as intended. He'd feel it was being stolen from him. I shivered, remembering the rest of what he'd said.

"You have a lot to lose. When I say that, I'm not just thinking of your marriage. I'm thinking of your brother." Gene didn't blink as he'd stared me down.

I called Dale, quickly checking in to make sure that Noah was okay. Dale said everything was fine: they'd been fishing that morning, and Chef was making chicken tenders for dinner along with hand-cut fries. Security was tight at the house because of the recent press situation.

But would security protect Noah against Gene Windsor?

I felt the walls closing in on me. *Mimi, Gene, Lydia...* oh my. I'd made a mess of things without even trying.

Before I could face filling out Gene's form, I scrolled through my calls to find Tate's number.

"Chloe?" She sounded wary. "Why're you calling me?"

"Because I wanted to know how it's going with Mimi. Did you tell her that Bryce and I were having problems?"

"Yeah, but she didn't seem really happy with me." Tate sighed. "She was pissed that you guys left. She's mad that her daughter doesn't seem to care too much, she's obsessed with some rocker dude. But it seems like Old Mimi's got all the time in the world, and she sure has an axe to grind."

"Can you tell me exactly what happened?" I needed to get Mimi managed somehow, some way.

"Why should I tell you anything, huh?" Tate asked. "She's the one who's paying me."

Ding ding ding. My conversation with Lydia came back to me. *I figured your husband might pay more...*

"Maybe I'm going to outbid her," I said, "but I'm not making any promises until I hear more."

"Hmm, okay." Tate sounded intrigued. "I told her that you and I were getting close and that things seemed rocky between you and Bryce, but she didn't seem satisfied. I get the feeling that she wants to blow your shit up. She's angry, huh? Somebody did something to her. She really hates this family."

I sighed. The fact that Daphne had slept with Mimi's husband, not to mention gotten pregnant, was obviously a huge issue. I hadn't helped matters by marrying Bryce and eliminating any possibility, no matter how small, of a reunion with Felicia. Then I'd gone and humiliated her daughter by beating the crap out of her at that wedding. *Way to go, Chloe.* How was I going to make this right?

"Tate, how did she find you?" I asked. I'd never

heard back from Elena about that. "How did she know about me?"

"She hired a private investigator—that's what she told me. And she found me on the *Sugar Finder* app. You were on there, right?"

"For a hot minute." The investigator must have found out that, somehow traced me to AccommoDating, and dug up Lydia's name and address, too.

"It worked out for you, huh?" Tate asked.

"I'm not sure about that just yet." My mind was racing. If Mimi had uncovered the details of my marriage to Bryce, Gene could do the same. He might have already.

"Did you mean what you said?" Tate broke through my panicked thoughts.

"About what?"

"About outbidding Mimi. And also, what you said about Colby before."

I shook my head, trying to clear it. "What did I say?"

"You said he thought he...liked me."

"I did mean it," I said immediately. "I wouldn't have said it otherwise."

Tate was quiet for a moment. Then she asked, "What about you outbidding Mimi, huh? Did you mean that?"

I hesitated. I'd *also* meant what I'd said about Mimi

Jones. But like Lydia, I would eventually have to put my money where my mouth was. That would involve explaining quite a few things to my husband.

Sometimes, the best defense was a good offense.

"I absolutely meant it. How much is she paying you?"

"Plenty. But there's always room for improvement," Tate said happily.

The next thing I did was text Midge and Hazel. *Please keep an eye on Tate,* I wrote. *She should start behaving better. If not, LMK?*

It was an odd feeling, texting Bryce's maid with the spindly legs. But what had I read during my junior-year Shakespeare class? *Misery acquaints a man with strange bedfellows.* I hadn't known what it meant until now!

Speaking of misery, I checked the clock. I had to upload Gene's dreaded form before my twenty-four hours ran out.

Fuck. What was I going to say? Attorney Finley had instructed me to include details about the board's proposed vote and Bryce's feelings about the position. What the hell was I supposed to tell Gene Windsor— the truth?

The board has lost faith in you. They want you out.

They're choosing Bryce over you.

He absolutely wants the job.

By the way, I signed a contract to marry your son. I worked for an escort agency. Mimi Jones knows all about it.

I might be pregnant...?

The last thought had me clutching my stomach. Between dealing with Lydia and Tate—and all the money I was promising everyone—I still hadn't taken the pregnancy test. I hustled upstairs to the bedroom, throwing my phone onto the bed. I grabbed the test from under the bathroom sink and read the instructions: pee on the stick and wait three minutes.

I took the test, set it on the counter, and ran back to my phone.

The board is voting on Bryce's appointment Monday morning. He's not sure how he feels about it, I wrote. I should stick as close to the truth as possible—Gene would be able to find out about the board's actions, anyway.

Bryce is doing the best he can. He cares so much about the company—he wants it to be successful. That was also the truth, but it probably wasn't what Gene was looking for.

What else could I tell him? How could I keep him at bay?

Mimi Jones has been sniffing around, I wrote. *She reached out to my stepmother, but I took care of it.*

There. At least that was something. Maybe it would occupy Gene's time, at least for a little while. I uploaded the form and cleared out the link.

As soon as I'd sent it, my phone pinged. It was a text message from a random five-digit number, which sent me to a link. *Click here for an encrypted message. This link will delete in five minutes.*

Hands shaking, I clicked the button.

You aren't cooperating with me and you know it.

You've told me nothing.

I already know about the board's plans, and I can more than handle the insufferable Mimi Jones.

If you don't provide more information about your husband, you are going to pay.

I know about you, Chloe. I know who you are and where you came from. Your father and his disgusting wife are on my payroll. They have no loyalty to you. They don't care if you live or if you die. They don't care about your brother.

I'm on the sidelines, but I'm still calling the plays.

I am in charge. I am in control.

Remember, I have eyes everywhere.

I also have people who will do what I say no matter what. I have the means to execute my plans, even from here.

Talk to Bryce tonight and send me more information.

Otherwise, you are going to be a very sorry young lady.

I ran to the bathroom and threw up.

As I sat on the floor, arms wrapped around myself, I glimpsed the pregnancy test on the counter. I got up, unsteady on my feet, and grabbed it.

There were two pink lines. *Pregnant.*

I should fill out the form again. I could just picture it. *Dear Gene, I almost forgot to tell you: your son's having a baby with his escort wife. The heir to Windsor Enterprises has a whore for a mother. What do you think about that?*

If I hadn't been scared sick, I would've laughed.

Instead, I promptly threw up again.

underdog

CHLOE

HAZEL, I wrote, *I know I'm not your favorite, but I need a favor. It's an emergency.*

I took a deep breath before I continued.

Please look out for my brother until I come home. You're close to the staff, no one knows more than you do about the comings and goings at the estate. Don't let anyone near Noah. Please talk to Dale about this! I'm calling him next.

Three dots immediately appeared. *Yes, Mrs. Windsor.* That was all she wrote, but I'd take what I could get.

I called Dale. God bless him, he picked up after one ring. "Dale, are you with Noah?"

"He's playing X-box in his room." Dale sounded worried. "What's the matter, Chloe?"

"I need you to stay with him. Make sure that no one... Make sure that no one takes him anywhere. I don't want him alone!" I wailed.

"Hold up. What the hell's going on?"

It was too risky to tell him the truth, so I made up a story about my father wanting custody. "I'm worried he might have reached out to Gene to ask for help—you know I'm not Gene's favorite. So don't leave him alone with any of the guys, okay? And get him a phone, tell him to keep it on him!"

"Okay, Chloe." But Dale didn't sound like he thought any of this was okay. "Does Bryce know what's going on?"

"Not yet. He's been with the board all day again."

"We've got him, Chloe. I won't let anything happen to your brother," Dale said.

"Hazel knows I'm worried. She's going to talk to you."

"You called *Hazel?* Okay, now I know you're serious. I'm going to call Bryce—"

"Let me do it first," I interrupted. "Let me talk to him when he gets home, okay? Now is not the time to bust him out of a meeting."

We hung up, and I paced the room, Gene's words rattling around in my head like a creepy skeleton.

I am in charge. I am in control.

... You are going to be a very sorry young lady.

Fuck! Why did Gene Windsor have to be so scary AND so rich? He was the puppet master from hell. Gene could hurt my brother. He could hurt Bryce. What the hell was I going to do?

My mind was going a million miles a minute when I got a call from Olivia Jensen. "What?" I snapped.

"Woah! Easy, Chloe." She laughed, a carefree sound, and I longed to leap through the phone and smack the public relations executive. "I'm just calling because I need more pictures. Can you meet Bryce downtown by the office? It would be good to have a shot of you two together in front of the building. My photographer's going to meet you there in an hour. Do your hair and makeup! Bryce already knows he needs to come down for a photo. Thanks, byeee!" She hung up without giving me a moment to protest.

Olivia Jensen and her PR initiative were so beside the point it was laughable. If only I could laugh. Instead, I dragged myself to the closet and dug out another insanely expensive outfit. I chose a deep-blue strapless dress and matching kitten heels, sexy but playful. If I got busted for being an escort, I should at least have some decent pictures on the internet! At least something better than the ones of me pummeling Felicia Jones...

I sat down in front of the enormous, well-lit mirror in the bathroom and started on my makeup. Was I imagining it, or did my complexion look good? Why did I look good if I kept throwing up? I stared at my reflection. Maybe it was because I knew I was pregnant, but I looked different.

Pregnant. I was carrying Bryce's baby... I rubbed my hand over my stomach, unable to even begin to process what this meant. Outside of all the drama swirling around me at the moment, what did I even think about the news? Honestly, I couldn't believe it. I'd gone from being a clueless virgin to being...

A clueless pregnant lady.

I should've known that having All The Sex with my husband—without birth control—would lead to this, but I hadn't even considered it! What on earth would my mother think? What would *Noah* think? I moved my hand up and placed it over my heart, which began thudding. *My brother has to be okay, please God, don't let anything happen to him! Mom, please watch over him...*

I was going to have to tell Bryce what was happening. But what would happen with Gene if I did that? Would he come after Bryce? Would he really try to take Noah from me—or even worse, hurt him?

Was Gene capable of something like that?

I didn't know the answer to that. I didn't want to find out.

I somehow managed to focus long enough to finish my makeup. I hustled downstairs, asked security to take me to the Financial District, and sent a quick message to Bryce. *Coming for the photo shoot. See you soon.*

I stared out the window, unseeing, as the lovely Beacon Hill townhomes flew by, then the bustling restaurants and high-rises of Back Bay. The driver took Massachusetts Avenue to the Financial District, and we sat in traffic for a few minutes. We passed through Downtown Crossing, still busy with shoppers, and I almost didn't recognize the city I'd grown up in.

Everything was different now. My whole life had changed that summer. It hadn't been that long ago that I'd met Elena for the first time in the North End. Starving, I'd shamelessly wolfed down the sandwich she'd bought for me. Desperate for money, I'd married a stranger.

Little had I known that he would be the key that unlocked me, opened me up, and brought meaning to my life.

I rubbed my stomach again. Things had changed, all right. Noah and I hadn't had enough money to eat after Lydia kicked us out. Now I was making cross-blackmail deals with my stepmother for millions of dollars. *I was* being blackmailed by my father-in-law, not to mention stupid Mimi Jones.

I tried to focus as we snaked through the traffic. What should I do? If I told Bryce the truth about his father, I risked Gene doing something terrible.

If I said nothing, I would continue to be beholden to him. And risked him doing something terrible.

I sighed and stared up at the sky, hoping to see the first star so I could make a wish. A wish for guidance, a wish for an answer, a wish for the right path.

But there was nothing up there but clouds.

moves

BRYCE

DALE TEXTED me during the meeting.

I need to talk to you. Important.

"Excuse me." I stood up from the table. Regina Hernandez gaped at me—she'd been mid-sentence. "I have to take this call. I'll be right back."

I headed outside, knowing that the board members would be worried. What was the emergency? Was it my father? My wife? When everything was in crisis, everything *seemed* like a crisis.

But my assistant never interrupted me. So even I was worried as I called him. "Dale? What's the matter?"

He sighed. "I don't want to speak out of turn, but your wife's worrying me."

"What do you mean?" My stomach churned.

"She called me a few minutes ago—she's worried about Noah."

"Okay..."

"She said she doesn't want him out of my sight. Is something going on? She even called Hazel."

"*What?*" My wife wasn't fond of the maid who'd been with me since I was a boy. And when I say she wasn't fond, I meant that she'd always seemed petrified of her. "Start talking, or I'm coming up there."

"I don't know what's wrong," Dale continued, "just that she said she doesn't want him alone with anyone. She said something about her father, that maybe he was trying to get custody back? And that she's worried *your* father might help him—"

"The hell? What is she talking about?" I raked a hand through my hair. Just then, Chloe texted that she was heading over for the impromptu photo shoot Olivia Jensen had organized. "She's on her way now. Listen, I don't know what's happening, but you absolutely have to watch Noah. Tell Hazel to stay with him. I'll call security and let them know we may have an issue."

I hung up and called Ted, my head guy. "Have you heard anything about a possible threat?"

"No, Mr. Windsor," he said. "There's been nothing unusual, except..."

"I'm listening. And remember, now that my father's gone, I'm in charge of everyone. And everything, including your paycheck."

Ted cleared his throat. "Mrs. Windsor— Mrs. *Daphne* Windsor—called earlier, she wanted to know who was on duty tonight."

"Who is on duty, Ted?"

"Patrick, Mike, and Leo. Is something wrong, Sir? I can't recall a time that Mrs. Windsor's made an inquiry like that."

"Nothing's wrong—thanks for your help." I didn't want to say too much, not yet.

I hung up and immediately texted Dale, telling him the names of the guards on duty. I asked him to find them in person, confiscate their phones, and let them know they were needed in an urgent meeting in half an hour.

Regina Hernandez flew out of the conference room. "Bryce, are you coming back?"

"Absolutely. But we need to take a break for dinner, don't you think? I'll send my assistant in to take everyone's orders. Do you want to order from the kitchen at The Four Seasons?" Regina loved The Four Seasons; she always stayed there for board business when she came into town.

"Sure." But she frowned as she eyed me. "Is everything okay?"

"Yes—I just have to meet my wife downstairs for a quick PR thing. Olivia hired a photographer. She thinks having a picture of us in front of the building would look good."

"Sounds like a great idea, Bryce. *Much* better than a picture of your wife getting into a fistfight. See you soon." She turned on her heel and was gone.

I was getting pretty sick of Regina Hernandez. If I got voted in as full CEO, she might find herself out on the sidewalk instead of in a cushy suite at The Four Seasons and in need of a new board gig...

We're parked out front, Chloe texted. I gave my assistant instructions for dinner—the team had been here since the sun came up, and I needed to keep them happy—then hustled to the elevator. What was going on with my wife? I remembered her tears from that morning, the odd vibe I'd gotten from her after we'd made love. And now she'd called Dale and *Hazel* and told them she was worried about Noah.

Something was definitely up. I could live with that, but it was a punch to the gut that she hadn't come to me first.

Was she planning on running again?

Over my dead body...

Chloe waited for me out on the sidewalk. She looked lovely in a strapless dress, her long, thick hair spilling over her shoulders. But something was off about her face—she looked different. She smiled for the camera, but the smile didn't go all the way to her eyes.

The photographer was instructing her to pose under the Windsor Enterprises sign. Chloe did as she was told, but she looked like a robot going through the motions.

Something was definitely wrong. But what the hell was it?

My heart started thudding as I went to her side. "You look pretty," I said, trying to maintain control over my emotions.

She sighed as she relaxed against me. "Thank you. You're a sight for sore eyes."

"You missed me, huh?" Heart still banging in my chest, I pulled her against me and smiled for the stupid photographer.

"Of course I did."

"You could've called." I couldn't help it: my tone turned accusatory.

Chloe glanced at me, eyes open wide, then looked away.

"Or is there some reason you didn't?" I plastered another fake smile onto my face as the photographer ushered us next to the building so he could get a different angle.

"I knew you were busy." Her tone sounded neutral and carefully controlled.

She was hiding something from me.

My palms started to sweat.

"I'm never too busy for you, Chloe." As the cameraman adjusted his equipment, I dropped the fake smile from my face. "I'd like to know what's going on with you."

"One more shot over by the entrance," the photographer called.

"I have to get back to my meeting," I snapped. I was out of patience after only five minutes. "Do you have something you can use?"

"Sure, Mr. Windsor. Thank you for your time."

I didn't bother to return the niceties as he headed for his van. I turned to my wife. A sick feeling swept through me, from my gut to my heart. "What's happening?"

She shook her head, still pretending. "What do you mean?"

"I think you know *exactly* what I mean." The sick feeling persisted; I wanted her to talk first. Would she reveal anything? Why was she worried about Noah? What was she planning?

My head thudded. And my heart...

I thought about the last time she'd left, how she'd blindsided me.

I couldn't go through that again—the surprise of it, the shock, how bad it hurt.

"Are you leaving me again?" The question tumbled out before I could control myself. I had to know.

Chloe took a step back. "What? No! Of course not. Bryce—"

"Let's go." I took her by the arm and headed for the SUV.

"Don't you have to get back to your meeting?"

"They can wait." I didn't look at her as I maneuvered her into the back seat. "Take us home, please."

I whipped out my phone and texted my assistant. *Tell them I had to deal with a staffing issue at home and that I'll be back. And make sure they have plenty to eat! Send in some wine and some bourbon,* I added as an afterthought. We would need to keep working for a few more hours. If they could relax a little, it would help. Maybe they'd drink so much they wouldn't notice I was gone.

Regina Hernandez wasn't going to be happy, but heading off another potential disaster with my wife would be better than more drama.

The driver slipped into the light traffic, taking a

right onto Federal Street and heading back through the city toward Beacon Hill.

"Dale called me earlier," I said.

"Oh?" Chloe didn't look at me. She seemed transfixed by the city lights flying by. "What's going on with him?"

My stomach flipped. *You're lying, Chloe.* "Why don't you tell me, huh?"

She sighed. "Why did you bring it up?"

"No reason." She wasn't offering anything, so I had to show her my cards. "But then I called the head of security and had a chat with him."

Chloe froze.

"He mentioned something about Daphne."

She whipped her head at me. "What? What about her?"

I shrugged.

"Bryce, tell me!" Her voice rose. "Tell me now!"

"Not until you tell me what you're afraid of."

"Please." She grabbed my hands. Her eyes were suddenly bright with unshed tears. "What did he say about Daphne?"

"She called security tonight."

"Fuck! Oh my god." Chloe whipped out her phone. Hands shaking, she scrolled through her contacts.

"Can you close the privacy screen, please?" she asked the driver.

She found Daphne's number, and as she was about to click it, she turned to me. "You are about to hear some shit. This could be the beginning of something bad. You need to know that."

"You're going to have to explain yourself—"

"I will, but you'll have to hold on." She didn't wait for me to answer, she just made the call.

I sat back, stymied, as I watched her.

"Daphne? I need to talk to you. Get your maid's phone and call me right back." She hung up, clutching her phone, waiting for it to ring. "Okay, I need you to go into one of the guest bathrooms and lock the door. Make sure no one follows you."

What the hell was going on? And who was this woman beside me? I'd never heard Chloe so commanding—or paranoid—in my life.

I could hear Daphne squawking on the other end of the line, probably complaining about using a maid's phone and being so thoroughly bossed around.

"Daphne, listen to me," Chloe interrupted. "I need to know something."

She hesitated for a moment. Her gaze skittered to me and away again. "How much is Gene paying you?"

Her brow furrowed as she listened. "Don't play dumb—I know you called security tonight."

Daphne squawked some more. Chloe took a deep breath and switched the phone to her opposite ear.

She grabbed my hand as she said, "We can do better than that. We can do *much* better than that. But I'm going to need you to switch teams."

TWENTY-THREE

the best defense

CHLOE

Once I made Daphne an offer she couldn't refuse, I gave her a caveat. "There's just one thing," I told her. "You can't go back to Gene for a counteroffer. If you do that, I'll make sure you don't see a dime from either of us, and I'll blow up your deal with Michael Jones, too. Don't screw me, Daphne. Believe me when I tell you that Bryce and I will be much better bosses than your evil husband."

She moaned. "He's going to lose it when I tell him I didn't do what he asked—"

"So don't tell him," I said firmly. "As far as Gene's concerned, everything's going forward as planned. I'm going to take care of everything, I promise. Just go to bed. We'll be back tomorrow, I'll wire you the money as soon as you set up a new bank account."

"Do you mean it?" she asked. "I'm taking a big risk if I do this."

"You can trust me—unlike your husband. You definitely can't trust him."

"True," she sighed. "What am I going to do, huh?"

"Pray he gets convicted, and then count your blessings. We're giving you so much money you'll be set for life. It won't matter if he stays in prison or not—you and the baby will be fine. I'll see you tomorrow, okay?"

After hanging up, I turned back to my husband. "I just promised her a crap ton of money."

He nodded. "I heard."

"And that's not the only deal I've made in the past twenty-four hours."

Bryce arched an eyebrow, and I sighed. "I've made a lot of commitments with your money—big ones. I'm so sorry, but I didn't know what else to do."

"Why don't you start by telling me what's happened?"

When I winced, he squeezed my hand. "I don't understand what's going on. And when I don't understand something, I'm afraid of it."

"Maybe you *should* be afraid." I wouldn't look at

him, I couldn't. If his father knew we were having this conversation right now, all hell would break loose. *My brother, my husband...* I was going to ruin everything. I didn't want that—I didn't want any of this. But what could I do?

"Is that because you want out?" Bryce stared straight ahead.

"What? *No!*" I squeezed his hand. "Bryce, look at me. That's the last thing that I want. All I want is to be with you, for us to be together."

His jaw was set; he looked like he was steeling himself against me, waiting for the final blow.

"This isn't about us—of course I don't want to leave. I love you. I will always love you." I clutched my stomach, feeling sick. "But I'm worried that I'm going to be the thing that ruins you."

He shook his head. "Not this again, Chloe—"

"No, listen." My voice was hoarse. "Your father hates me. That's why I left the first time. He wanted me gone. He'll never think I'm worthy of being a Windsor."

"I don't care what my father thinks. I never have, and I never will. Especially not when it comes to you."

I swallowed hard. "T-Thank you. But he's taken it one step further than thinking. He's threatened me. Actually, he's not even threatening *me*—he's threatened to hurt you. And Noah. He said he'd hurt my brother."

I broke down, the tears spilling over as I realized what I'd done. I'd finally gone and broken my promise to Gene, and now I was going to pay. "I c-can't lose my brother, if something happened—"

But Bryce was already on the phone. "Dale? Get the guards together *now*. Call the Chief and have him come, too. I want everyone's phones—no one's allowed to make a call, no one's allowed off the island, *nothing*. Do you understand? Call me as soon as you have them together."

He hit the intercom button to talk to the driver. "I need you to turn around and get us back to the office right now."

"Yes, Mr. Windsor." He took a hard right, and I held onto my seat.

"Okay, this is what we're going to do." Bryce gripped my hand. "We're going in to meet with the board right now. I'm going to make sure that anyone still holding out hope that my father's coming back understands that's not going to happen and that his era is over *now*. Then we're going home."

"Tonight?"

He nodded. "As soon as we leave the meeting. I'm not going to let anything happen to our family, Chloe. My father's lucky he's safe in jail because otherwise, I might kill him."

"I'm worried *he's* going to do something like that. I'm worried he's going to try to hurt you or Noah. That's what he said he would do if I told you, that's why I left the first time, he doesn't want us to be together, he doesn't want you to take over and push him out—"

"He doesn't get to say anymore. It's not his life, and it's not his company. I'm taking over and going to legal with all of this. We'll blow him up once and for all, Chloe." He turned to me. "Thank you for finally showing me how."

"What? I don't understand."

He put his arm around me. "Just stay with me, okay? We're going to do this—and everything else—together."

We parked back in front of the building and hustled inside. The elevator silently whisked us upstairs, and Bryce grabbed my hand as we entered the boardroom together. Well-dressed, fatigued-looking men and women gaped at us from the conference table.

"You're not The Four Seasons delivery guy," one of the men joked.

"No, I'm not." Bryce shut the door behind us and pulled up a chair for me. Before I sat, he put his arm around me again. "I'd like to formally introduce my wife, Chloe Windsor. She'll be joining us for the next part of the meeting."

Regina Hernandez cleared her throat. "That's rather unorthodox, Bryce. We have a standard non-disclosure agreement she needs to sign if you want her to stay."

"She'll sign it after," he snapped. "And I want to say something to you."

He sat back and eyed the other board members. "To all of you."

They waited, suddenly looking a lot more alert.

"No matter what happens with me as CEO of Windsor Enterprises—whether I remain on as interim, become permanent, or someone else comes on board— my father will not be returning to a leadership role here."

Murmurs broke out, and he held up his hand. "Before I say more, I want you to know that we're aware that some of you have been providing him with information that's considered confidential. I understand many of you have worked with Gene for a long time and that your allegiance is to him. I also know that he can be difficult and vindictive, and sometimes he's willing to pay for loyalty. That stops tonight."

Bryce straightened his shoulders. "I know who has been supplying him with details, and for the record, I am willing to let it go. But it ends now, at this meeting. If anyone leaks this conversation to him, I will make sure you're prosecuted to the full extent of the law, fired from the board, and, just for fun, publicly humiliated."

He let that sink in before he continued. "That being said, if you feel you can't serve the board under this new set of circumstances, leave now."

No one moved.

"Great. Anyone who stays and remains loyal to the board, its mission, and our confidentiality agreement will receive a bonus. My father might be willing to pay for loyalty, but it turns out, so am I. And I happen to be much more generous. So if you stay, everyone will be getting a salary increase to seven figures per year. That's a one-hundred percent jump." Bryce grinned at them. "For a side gig, I'd say that's a pretty good payout."

The board members gaped at him. After a moment, Regina Hernandez raised her hand. "Bryce, I'd like to say something."

"I'm listening." He didn't sound happy about it.

"First of all, I'm sorry I made that comment about the picture of Chloe fighting at your cousin's wedding."

Bryce nodded, and I inwardly sighed. I was never going to live that down!

"Second, I am *thrilled* that we're doing this," Regina continued. "I'm so glad you're showing your true leadership skills. Your father has been a toxic influence on the company for a long time. He's stifled our innovation and limited our philanthropic partnerships. And like you said, he's difficult and vindictive. He's made it hard to vote against him."

Regina smiled at the other board members. "I'd like to bring Bryce Windsor's appointment to full-term CEO to a vote. All of those in favor say aye."

The vote was unanimous. Bryce was no longer an interim: he was the real deal.

He stood, accepting warm congratulations all around. "We are not making this announcement public until Monday afternoon. I have some personal business I need to attend to before we do that. Is everyone clear?"

Again, the response was unanimous.

"I think they liked that pay raise," I whispered to Bryce as we rode the elevator down.

He winked at me. "You inspired me, Chloe."

"I did?"

"The way you convinced Daphne so quickly got me thinking: people need to be motivated to make a change. It helped me see my situation with the board differently." Bryce smiled. "Guess I'm not the only CEO in the family."

Warmth bloomed inside my chest. "Huh. I guess not."

"You still have some things you need to tell me, though."

I sighed. "Yeah, I do. Can I ask you a question first?"

He gave me the lopsided grin that I loved. "Sure."

"How much money do you really have?"

Bryce laughed. "A lot. I have a lot."

"Good" Relief flooded me. "Because I think there are even more people we need to pay off."

TWENTY-FOUR

negotiations

CHLOE

BEFORE WE GOT on the plane, Bryce called Dale again. "We'll be there in an hour. Don't let anyone in or out."

He turned to me. "I'm calling Hazel."

He put the maid on speakerphone. "Are you with Noah?"

"Yes, Mr. Windsor." There were loud noises in the background, some kind of music mixed with the dog barking. "We're keeping ourselves entertained."

"What are you doing? And are you safe?"

"We're quite safe, I can assure you," Hazel said. "All of the staff, Chef included, are watching young Mr. Burke's room. Midge and the other girls are camped outside. And we are inside, teaching the dog to roll over and playing some sort of game."

The sound became muffled for a moment. "Noah—what's this called again? Ah, yes. We're playing *Fortnite*. Unfortunately, I'm quite awful at it."

"You're not that bad, Hazel!" Noah piped up. "I mean, you've died, like, seven thousand times, but at least you're not giving up. You know who's really awful at video games? Bryce. He sucks!"

"All right, all right," Bryce said, but he was laughing. "Stay with him, Hazel. There's no one I trust more than you."

"Mr. Windsor... Thank you." She sounded genuinely touched.

"If anyone needs a raise, it's probably Hazel," I said when he hung up.

"You know what? You're right."

We were quiet on the quick plane ride. The city lights from Boston dimmed, and the northern New England states were dark and sleepy beneath us. Maine was peaceful and quiet as we landed, the land hushed around us as we drove through the dark mountains to Northeast Harbor.

My phone pinged with a text. *Click here for a secure link.*

I swallowed hard. "I think your father knows I'm not in Boston anymore. He just sent me a message."

Bryce's expression turned stormy. "Open it."

I clicked on the link with shaking hands, petrified that someone on the board had already ratted us out. Instead, there were several pictures of the primary-suite bathroom at Bryce's house on Beacon Hill. "What the hell?"

I clicked through them, then clutched my stomach.

The final picture was of the inside of the wastepaper basket. It was my discarded pregnancy test, two pink lines clearly showing. "Oh my God."

This is never going to happen, read the caption below the last picture. That was all Gene wrote.

I clutched the phone to my chest and curled in on myself.

"What the hell did he say?" Bryce sounded on the verge of exploding.

"Bryce... I need to tell you something."

He put his face in his hands.

"It's nothing bad. I mean, *I* don't think it's bad," I babbled. "I'm... I'm pregnant."

"What?" He sat up straight. "What did you just say?"

"I'm pregnant. As in, I am carrying your baby in my

stomach. I think? Or am I carrying it in my uterus...?" It had been some time since I'd attended health class.

"Oh my God. Chloe, I can't. I... What? Wow." His eyes brightened until he saw my hands still curled around my phone. "What the hell did my father say?"

"He knows somehow. Someone at the house must've gone through my trash—they sent him a picture."

"Let me see it." His voice was ice.

"I don't think that's a good idea—"

He wrenched the phone from my hands, scrolling through the pictures until he reached the end. I could tell when he'd read the caption because it looked like smoke might pour out of his ears. Bryce's expression changed several times as he processed what Gene had said. It went from rage to disbelief to disgust.

"I can't believe he's my father."

"Bryce..." I took a deep breath. "I'm the last person who'd defend him, but he's had everything taken from him. Of course he's lashing out. He knows that his life isn't ever going to be the same, he's desperate."

"Good." My husband stared straight ahead. "He deserves everything that's coming to him."

I sighed and sat back against the seat. "I'm sorry I didn't tell you sooner. I just took the test—I've been in shock. With everything else going on, it really threw me for a loop."

"Are you..." He hesitated. "Are you okay with it?"

"What? I'm—Bryce, I'm thrilled." I blinked at him. "How do *you* feel?"

"Are you kidding me?" His face opened up into a grin, and it was like the sun coming out. "I'm the happiest man in the world. Except for the fact that my father's trying to destroy my family."

"About that. There are some other people involved, too. It's not just Daphne."

Again, it looked like smoke was about to pour out of Bryce's ears. "Tell me everything. We have ten minutes until we get to the dock."

I took a deep breath. "First of all, like I said, we have several new people on the payroll. My stepmother's one of them."

"Lydia? We just gave her money! What the hell does she want now?"

"More. And I promised her more. Like, a lot more," I admitted.

"Why did we do that?"

At least Bryce said 'we.' That meant he couldn't be completely mad at me!

"Because someone else was paying her—actually, two different people were—and I had to offer more."

He scrubbed a hand over his face. "Who? Tell me everything."

I sighed. "Your father, and also, Mimi Jones."

"What? Why the hell is Mimi Jones blackmailing Lydia?"

"She wasn't blackmailing her, she was trying to get her to do things. Like bring a local news crew to the townhouse and embarrass me." I shook my head. "Mimi thinks I should be ashamed of my father and Lydia, and so does your father. And I *am* ashamed of them, but not for the reasons you might think."

"It's because of how they treated you and Noah," Bryce said.

"Right." I shrugged. "I don't care that Lydia chain-smokes and has a giant tattoo of a lion's face on her thigh. If she was a nice person, I'd be all for it. But she's not. She's not a nice person, and I offered her a *lot* of money not to talk. I mean, a lot."

Bryce waved his hand. "We'll worry about that later. What else? Tell me more about Mimi. I don't understand how she's involved in all of this."

"Ugh, there *is* more. She hates our family. She's so bitter about what happened with Michael and Daphne that she's taking it out on us. And the fact that you and Felicia didn't work out doesn't help matters. But really, she hates *me*." I shivered. "I never should've gone after

Felicia at the wedding. That was your father's idea to make me look bad."

"I freaking *knew it*—"

"It doesn't matter. Because not only did I embarrass myself, I humiliated the Jones family. And I think Mimi was already humiliated enough—that pushed her over the edge."

I blew out a deep breath. "Mimi was disgusted that she wasn't able to keep that out of the news, and now the most famous picture of her precious American-heiress daughter is the one of her getting her ass kicked by Nobody Chloe Windsor. Who's an escort. Who's stepmother is East Boston trash with an accent and a huge thigh tattoo."

"Jesus Christ." Bryce looked appalled. "Mimi needs to get a life."

"She knows about AccommoDating, Bryce. She told Lydia about it. Your father knows, too."

I paused for a beat, letting that sink in. Our enemies knew the truth about us. What on earth were we going to do about *that*?

"I guess she hired a private investigator to dig up my past and whoever it was, they did good work," I continued. "Oh, that's the other thing—Mimi's the one who hired Tate to go after your brother. Tate's an escort, too. She's been threatening me ever since she got to the island."

"What the *hell*? I'm going to have security pack her shit and throw her out—"

"No, no you can't do that!" I interrupted. "Tate's on the payroll, too. I told her to lie to Mimi and keep things on an even keel while we figure out our next move. She's not that bad, actually. I feel sorry for her, she was living on the streets before she started working as an escort. And she really likes Colby."

Bryce looked at me as though I had three heads.

"What?"

"You seem to empathize with my father, even though he's been torturing you. You feel sorry for Tate, even though she threatened you. You don't even sound like you hate Mimi, and she's trying to blow your life up." His brow furrowed. "How do you do that?"

"How do I do what?"

"Stay good. How do you stay so good, huh?"

I shook my head. "I'm *not* good. But enough people have tried to do bad things to me since I married you, I don't know... I guess I see it from a different perspective. Like, why sink to their level? Although I'm all about the payoffs, and I learned that from watching *them*."

I laughed. "But I just figure, why can't the good guys win for once? We—*you*—have a ton of money, just like your dad and Mimi. Why can't we throw some of that around and come out on top?"

"We can, Mrs. Windsor. We absolutely can." He grinned at me. "But we have some serious ass to kick first. Are you with me?"

I laced my fingers through his. I was still afraid—afraid for my brother, afraid for Bryce and his position with the company, fearful of all of it—but for the first time in a long time, I felt lighter.

For better or for worse, I'd told my secrets. What was it my mother used to say? *Sunlight is the best disinfectant.* I felt better—cleaner—for telling him the truth.

"I'm with you. There's no place I'd rather be."

Now I just had to pray for more time.

trust

CHLOE

Captain Johnny seemed concerned on the boat ride to the island. "Dale said there was a security threat—is everything okay?"

"It is. It will be." Bryce hesitated for a moment. "We've had some issues in the family, Johnny. You've been with us for a long time, so I'm sure you're not surprised by that."

The captain nodded as he carefully steered through the buoys in Northeast Harbor.

"I know your father was upset before he was taken into custody. It was an open secret among the staff, Sir. He'd been complaining about you boys. If you asked me, he seemed paranoid that he would lose his significance within the company." He shrugged. "Just my two cents."

"You're absolutely right." Bryce nodded. "That's exactly what he was worried about, and he's taken some steps to protect himself that I don't think are very...respectable. I need to ask you something. I want you to know that I won't hold it against you—I know how my father can be."

Captain Johnny's grip tightened on the steering wheel. "Go ahead, Mr. Windsor. I don't have anything to hide."

"Did my father ever approach you? Before he went to prison, I mean. I believe he was trying to get some of the employees to spy on Chloe and me."

The captain nodded. "He made the rounds, Mr. Windsor. But as far as I know, no one ever accepted his offers. We were all very cordial to him, of course. Your father could be difficult, you know that. He wasn't an easy man to say no to, but I think he also knew that everyone here loved the family. We're loyal to the *Windsors*, you know? Not just him. He didn't ever make a scene about it, as far as I know."

"So, to your knowledge, no one on the staff was spying for him?"

"I did hear one thing." The older man's face clouded.

"What?"

He sighed. "I didn't believe it, though. She's not popular with a lot of the staff because she's so set in her ways and so particular. I thought they were just gossiping—"

"About who?" My voice was shrill. "Who are you talking about?"

Captain Johnny glanced back at me. "Hazel, Mrs. Windsor. There was a rumor that she was spying for the other Mr. Windsor."

I felt like I might pass out.

"I'm going to need you to go as fast as you can," Bryce instructed. "We need to get to the island immediately. It's an emergency."

"Yes, Sir."

The engine roared, and the yacht picked up speed, but to me, time had stopped. *Hazel was working for Gene Windsor. Hazel was alone with my brother in his room...*

"It can't be true," Bryce murmured. "I don't believe it.."

It seemed to take forever, but we reached the dock. Bryce and I jumped from the boat and ran up to the house. "I want you to stay downstairs," he panted, but I shoved him out of the way.

"It's my brother!" Tears were already streaming down my face. "I need to save him!"

"Mr. and Mrs. Windsor, what's the matter?" Chef

practically jumped out of the way as we flew through the house and took the stairs two by two. Midge and several other maids were camped out in the hallway, playing cards.

"Chloe!" She sprang to her feet. "What's the matter?"

But I flew past her and threw open my brother's door.

Noah and Hazel were sitting cross-legged on the floor, a bowl of cheese puffs between them, hollering at the television.

"Take that, Renegade Raider!" Hazel's thumbs clicked furiously on the controller. "I've got you now!"

"Dude!" Noah wailed. "You're shooting backward! I told you—"

"Noah!" I threw myself at him, spilling the cheese curls. "Are you okay?"

"Let go of me!" He wrenched free and peered over my shoulder at the screen. "Thanks a lot, Chloe, you just killed me. What's the matter with you, huh?"

Hazel rose to her feet, her knees cracking.

"Mr. Windsor, Mrs. Windsor." She looked at me, obviously concerned, as I clutched my brother. "Has something happened?"

"We need to speak with you, Hazel." Bryce

motioned for my brother. "Stay outside with Midge. Don't go anywhere."

"Seriously? I just lost my game!" Noah huffed as he left the room. "Don't go anywhere, Hazel. We need a rematch."

Bryce closed the door behind him, then turned to the maid. "I need to ask you something, and I'm sorry to have to do it."

"What's this about, Mr. Windsor?"

Bryce sighed. "Someone told me that you'd accepted a bribe from my father. Did he ask you to spy on us?"

Hazel bowed her head. "Yes, Mr. Windsor. He did."

"And did you do it?"

"Not exactly." Hazel dug into the pockets of her uniform, revealing a small zipped bag. "Here." She handed it to Bryce.

He looked perplexed as he opened it and pulled out a wad of hundred-dollar bills. "You took his money?" Bryce sounded crushed.

Hazel raised her gaze to meet his. "Yes, Mr. Windsor. And I told him that I would spy for him. But I was only doing it to protect you. I only told him lies. And I planned to turn the money over to you, to put it into a trust for the boy."

"For Noah?"

She nodded. "I wasn't very kind to Mrs. Windsor when she first arrived here—I didn't trust her intentions. Ever since you were a boy, I've been protective of you, Mr. Windsor. So I treated Mrs. Windsor too harshly."

She peered past Bryce to me. "I believe she has your best interests at heart, Mr. Windsor. And I think you know me well enough to recognize that I would never be loyal to anyone but you. I did this to protect you. And I kept the money for the boy because I know what it feels like not to have parents looking out for you."

She dropped her gaze. "If you feel it's necessary to terminate me because I didn't reveal this to you, I understand."

"Aw Hazel, c'mon." Bryce surprised all of us by sweeping her into his arms for a hug. She yelped, and he quickly released her. "You've been like a mother to me since my mom passed. I'm giving you a raise. I'm going to buy you a house wherever you want."

"I only ever wanted to stay here and be of service."

He smiled at her. "Then you can stay here and be of service. But I'm sending you on a trip someplace nice. All expenses paid, five-star all the way. How does that sound?"

For the first time ever, I saw Hazel crack a smile. "That sounds lovely, Mr. Windsor."

I stepped forward. "Hazel, thank you for looking out

for Noah while we were gone. And thank you for setting that money aside for him." I was touched by her gesture. "I think Noah was really having fun hanging out with you. Is it okay if you stay with him a little longer? Bryce and I have some business to take care of."

"Of course, Mrs. Windsor. It would be my pleasure."

I brought my brother back in, and he immediately coerced her back to the floor. He handed her a cheese curl and an x-box controller. "We're totally gonna win this game."

"You know what? I think you might be right." Hazel popped the cheese curl into her mouth and chose her Fortnite skin—a female Viking warrior wearing a pink-bunny backpack.

"Thanks again, Hazel." I was so lucky that my brother was surrounded by good people. "See ya, Noah."

"Smell you later," he said. "Hazel, look out for the storm! It's coming in hot!"

I shook my head as we left them. Midge and the others were waiting for us, worried expressions on their faces.

"Is everything okay?"

"What's going on?"

"Why does Dale have the security team locked in the conference room?"

"Are we safe? Is Noah okay?"

Bryce held up his hand. "Everything's going to be fine, and yes, we are all safe here. Noah's safe. Thank you all for your continued patience with me and your dedication to the family. Everyone's getting raises—big raises."

"Ooh, yay!" Midge's eyes glittered. "I'm going to help my niece pay for grad school!"

"I'll pay for it. It's on me." Bryce smiled. "Does anyone know where my brothers are?"

"Jake's in the study. I think Colby's at the guest-house with Tate?"

"Thanks, ladies. Stay here until everything's finalized, okay? I'll have Chef send up some appetizers and some wine."

They were all smiles and good cheer.

"Thank you, Mr. Windsor!"

"That's so nice of you!"

"We're so glad you guys are back!"

We hustled down the stairs, and Bryce whipped out his phone. "Jake, I need you to meet me outside the conference room. Yes, right now."

He called Colby next. "I need you at the house. Bring the girl."

We stopped in the hallway, and he turned to me. "Are you ready for the next act?"

I took a deep breath. "I hope so."

He nodded. "Just remember, we're coming out of this on top. No matter what."

He held out his hand and I clung to him for dear life. "I hope you're right."

"Babe." Bryce smiled. "I don't like to flaunt it, but... I'm always right."

"Ha!"

"I was right about you." He leaned in for a kiss. "Now let's just hope that luck holds out a little longer."

coming clean

BRYCE

I'D SAID I was usually right about everything, which was true. But one thing I'd done wrong? I'd let my little brothers get away with too few responsibilities. I'd shielded them from my father, bearing the brunt of his moods and accusations while letting Jake and Colby play.

But now their houses of sticks and straw were about to be blown down by none other than moi.

Jake showed up first. "What's up? I was just on the phone with Dubai."

"We need to talk."

He eyed Chloe. "Hi Chloe. Are you joining us?"

"You're joining *us*," I corrected him. "We're waiting for Colby. And Tate."

Jake raised his eyebrows at the mention of Colby's girlfriend but said nothing. Colby and Tate hustled in a minute later, both in their sweats. "We were working out," Colby said. "What's so urgent?"

"I'll tell you in there." Bryce motioned to the conference room. "Heads up, Dale's in there with the security team. We're having a meeting with them."

"Why?" Colby asked. He turned to Tate and Chloe. "Why don't you guys go wait in the kitchen?"

"They're coming in with us. Tate, I'm going to need you to sign something." Bryce got on his phone. "Jim? It's me. I'm going to need you to send over a non-disclosure agreement immediately. She can fill out the personal details, and you can make it all pretty and official. Thanks."

"Why is Tate signing an NDA?" Colby looked wary.

"Because of what we're about to discuss." His phone pinged, and he handed it to Tate. "Please fill out your name and legal address, and sign it where the tab is."

"Permanent address?" Tate looked concerned. "I don't really have one."

"You can use mine, babe." Colby recited his address.

That seemed to perk her up. "Thanks, babe."

Jake and Bryce looked at each other, then looked away.

After she'd signed, Bryce knocked on the conference door, and we headed in. The meeting seemed tense. Dale stood at the front of the room while Ted, the lead security guard, paced the back.

Ted's cheeks were flushed. "Mr. Windsor, finally! My men have been in here for hours! We haven't been on patrol, their phones have been confiscated—"

"Have a seat, Ted. We need to have a frank discussion, and I'm the one who'll be doing the talking."

"Yes, Sir." Ted sat down immediately.

"I need you all to know that as of tonight, my father is no longer the one in charge. I'm taking over as head of Windsor Enterprises. The board voted on it earlier this evening. My appointment's effective immediately."

"What?" Colby's eyes almost popped out of his head.

"Does Dad know?" Jake looked stunned.

"Congratulations," Dale said. "I expect a raise!" He laughed until Bryce glared at him, and then it turned into a cough.

Bryce faced the rest of the group. "I understand that Mrs. Windsor—the *other* Mrs. Windsor—was in touch with some of you tonight, looking for information about Noah. I need you to understand that Noah is part of our family, and you have to protect him. He's a Windsor, now."

Bryce looked at each man in turn. "I need your absolute loyalty moving forward. I understand that my father has made several offers in order to secure information and possibly, other actions."

Bryce let that sink in for a moment. "I'm aware of this, and I'd like to say I understand. My father can be persuasive. But any of those preexisting relationships? They end now. I'm canceling your previous contracts and offering new ones. I'm doubling your salaries, and I'm offering generous signing bonuses—more than whatever my father was offering any of you. Does anyone have any objections?"

There were no objections, only smiles, and relief. I wasn't the only one who hated being Gene Windsor's bitch!

"My legal team will prepare the documents—so for now, you can get back to work. I need everyone to be on high alert, though. My father is being frozen out, and he's going to react. As of right now, he's unaware of the changes taking place. But I don't know how long that will last. So everyone, please be safe, and keep my family safe. That will be all."

The team filed out, and Bryce turned to the rest of us. "Now it's time for real family talk. Who's excited?"

Jake scratched behind his ear. Colby bounced on the balls of his feet.

Tate raised her hand. "Why am I here, exactly?" Her gaze flicked to Chloe.

Bryce put his arm around me. "Because we're having a family meeting, and you are currently dating a Windsor. If Colby wants you here on the island, you need to be in this meeting. Colby?"

"I'd like you to stay, Tate." Colby smiled at her. "I mean, we're basically living together."

"Okay, babe." But Tate sounded nervous.

"Bonus points if you stop saying 'babe,'" Jake huffed.

Colby nudged him good-naturedly. "Whatever you say, babe."

"Enough, guys." Bryce turned to me. "Chloe and I have something to tell you. Several somethings. Chloe?"

"Oh... Okay. Wow, we're doing this?" Chloe held onto me for dear life.

"Go ahead, honey. I'm right here."

She took a deep breath. "I didn't meet Bryce at Dunkin' Donuts. We didn't tell you the truth about how we got together. The story was much more complicated than that."

"Oh." Now it was my turn to hang onto *her*. "This is what we're telling them?"

"This is the first thing," she said bravely. She faced my brothers and Tate. "The thing is, I worked for an agency. An escort agency. And Bryce found me through them—that's how we met. Your father knows the truth about me, and he isn't happy. I mean, he wasn't happy anyway. Hey." She turned back to me. "Shouldn't Daphne be here? She needs to hear this, and I don't want to have to say it all again."

I called Daphne and asked her to join us immediately. Then I poured myself a bourbon and one for my brothers.

"Are you old enough to drink?" I asked Tate.

"I'm pretty sure I need one, regardless." She knocked it back in one shot, and I felt a little sorry for her.

Daphne bustled in, eyes bright. She glanced at Chloe. "Having a family meeting without me? I thought we had a deal!"

"We do," Chloe assured her. "As soon as I realized we were doing this, I had Bryce call you. I told you that you can trust me, and I meant it."

Jake and Colby watched this exchange with interest. "You two have a side deal?" Jake asked.

Chloe nodded. "I'll explain everything in a minute."

Tate poured herself another bourbon.

"Daphne, I was just telling everyone about my background. But first, Bryce let them know that he was voted in as full-term CEO of Windsor Enterprises earlier tonight."

Daphne sat down and fanned herself. "Thank God I decided to accept your offer. Otherwise I'd be out pawning Gene's original art on the internet as we speak."

"I'm glad you're here." Chloe smiled at her, but then it faltered. "I have to bring you up to speed though, Daphne. I was just telling everyone about how Bryce and I met. It wasn't the way that I told you."

She hesitated before she continued. "I met Bryce through a...dating...agency. An escort agency, actually. And Gene knows about it, and so does Mimi Jones."

Daphne's mouth formed an 'O.' "Wow, I had no idea."

My wife arched an eyebrow. "It's not exactly the sort of thing you'd guess."

"It's like *Pretty Woman*." Daphne shook her head as if to clear it. "I feel so much better about thinking you were trash at first!"

"Gee Daphne, tell me how you really feel," Chloe groaned.

Daphne's eyes sparkled. "I like you now."

"I like you, too—God help me." Chloe shook her head. "The thing is, Gene's been blackmailing me. He never wanted me to stay married to Bryce. He's the reason I did that stupid morning talk show interview, got into that fight with Felicia Jones, and left in the middle of the night. He threatened me, he threatened my brother, and he's threatened Bryce."

"He did the same thing to me, Chloe." Daphne nodded. "He said he'd blow up my deal with Michael Jones, void our pre-nuptial agreement so I got nothing, and divorce my ass. He said he would sabotage my company if I didn't do what he wanted. And the last thing he asked me to do was find out what guards were on duty while you were gone. I bet that was because he was going to try to take Noah."

Chloe shuddered. "He had a deal with my father and stepmother—he might've been trying to give Noah back to them. At least, I hope that's all he was trying to do."

Both Colby and Jake looked uneasy.

"Did Dad approach you, too?" I asked my brothers.

Jake blew out a deep breath. "He promised me a bigger share of the company if I worked against you, Bryce. I said I would do it just to keep him happy, but I didn't mean it. I would never do anything to hurt you, I hope you know that."

Colby shrugged. "All he offered me was an additional three million and the golf courses he owns. I said yes, of course."

When Jake and I started protesting, he held up his

hands. "I didn't tell him anything! I wouldn't do that. But I *did* want those golf courses."

"You can keep them." I laughed. "The legal team thinks Dad's definitely going to jail. If that's the case, the emergency provisions of the trust kick in. And guess who's the trust administrator?"

I pointed to myself. "This guy. Golf courses for everyone!"

The mood lifted in the room until Chloe cleared her throat. "There's more—good news and other news. What do you want first?"

"The good news," Colby said immediately.

Chloe moved closer to me, and hot pride bloomed in my chest. "Bryce and I are having a baby."

"Shut up!" Daphne sprung out of her chair and pulled Chloe in for a hug. "Our babies are going to grow up together! We can buy them matching Chanel onesies! Oh my God, this is the best news ever!"

"Gene doesn't know yet. He won't be thrilled, but we are."

My brothers hugged me, and Tate raised her glass to us in a toast. Still, I could tell she was nervous. She knew that the gig was up; she was obviously the 'other news.'

"The last thing we need to tell you pertains to Tate." I nodded at her. "Would you like to speak for yourself?"

"Not really." She drained her glass. "But here goes

nothing. Colby, I'm an escort, too. Mimi Jones hired me to get involved with you and...infiltrate the family." Her cheeks heated. "Chloe's known about it for a while because I threatened her—that's what Mimi was paying me to do."

Tate's face was turning red; Colby's face was turning white. "What? I don't understand."

"I lied to you," she said, her voice low. "The stuff I told you about my background, it was all made up. Mimi found me on a dating app, and she hired me to come up here. I wanted to tell you the truth so many times, but I couldn't do it..."

"This whole thing has been a *job*?" My little brother looked sick.

"It started that way." Tate shrugged. "But then I fell for you, and I, like, don't even hate Chloe enough to do mean things to her. She's been nice to me, even when I was a total bitch. She offered to pay me instead of Mimi so I'd stop working for her."

"You've known about this for a while?" Colby turned to my wife.

She nodded.

"Why the hell didn't you tell me?"

"I'm so sorry." Chloe's shoulders slumped. "But I didn't say anything because I was worried about myself, my brother—and *Bryce*. Tate threatened to go public about my background. I couldn't have that blowing up in my face when your father was already out to get me. I hope you can forgive me."

Colby scrubbed a hand over his face while Tate frowned. "I guess it's too much for *me* to ask you for forgiveness, huh?"

"I don't know. I don't know anything right now." Colby looked up at me. "Except that I'm glad you're in charge. Dad did a lot of bad stuff. He's not a bad guy, but he's done a lot of bad things. It's time for a change."

Jake nodded. "All of this has been hard, but that's how this stuff goes, right? Everything's falling into place. It's been rough, but we're still here. That means something, I guess."

I poured another round of bourbons. Tate joined in, too, although Colby definitely gave her some space. Chloe and Daphne raised their glasses of water.

"To still being here."

That was something. That was everything.

worthy

CHLOE

I CHECKED THE CLOCK—IT was almost time. Olivia Jensen had pulled a rabbit out of a hat and made arrangements for that very morning.

I couldn't believe I was doing this again.

And this time would be so, so much worse. Because this time, I was going to have to tell the truth. About myself. To millions of people. On national television.

I closed my eyes and said a quick prayer. *Mom, I hope you know I did all this for a good reason. I promise I'll always take care of him.*

"Why're you crying!" Midge swatted me with a tissue. "Is it the hormones?"

Midge was even more excited than Daphne about

my pregnancy. She'd only known for twelve hours, but somehow she'd already started a Pinterest board of possible outfits, baby names, and nursery decorating ideas.

"I'm nervous," I admitted.

"Don't be. You're protecting your family. What's that saying? Sunlight is the best disinfectant." Midge smiled at me.

"Aw! My mom used to say that."

Midge winked as she started working on my lip gloss. "Your mom was a smart lady."

I nodded. "She was." *I hope you forgive me for going on Sugar Finder, Mom!*

"And because she was a smart lady, she'll understand why you made the choices you did. I bet she's up in heaven right now, really proud of you."

"I hope so." My eyes pricked with tears again.

"I *know* so—okay, stop!" Midge forced another tissue on me. "I have to get you downstairs!" She finished with my makeup, insisted that I wear a body-hugging dress and sky-high heels, and then sent me on my way.

Olivia Jensen waited at the landing, clutching her signature enormous iced coffee. She was the one person on the staff that didn't know the truth yet. We didn't want her leaking information to the press or worse, running to Gene.

As always, the PR executive looked pulled together, her makeup perfect, a cute ivory adorning her curvy figure. "You look great—your skin's glowing," she said. "How are you feeling?"

"Nervous," I admitted. "Was the network surprised we reached out?"

"They were thrilled, to tell you the truth. They want the inside scoop on how the family's doing now that Gene's in prison." Olivia led me downstairs to the media room. The camera crew had arrived at four a.m. to get everything set up. Once again, the morning talk show hosts were going to interview me live from New York via a video chat. The same production crew and assistant had returned to the island to run things on our end.

We headed inside the media room, which was buzzing with the production crew. There were lights and cameras all over the place, barely organized chaos. "They're going to want to know how Bryce is holding up. They will probably ask you about the fight with Felicia Jones, even though I asked them not to."

"Ugh. Do I have to talk about that?" The fight seemed like it happened in another lifetime when the pretty heiress had been my biggest worry. My, how times had changed!

Olivia sighed. "They agreed to do this interview at the last second. I think we owe them the courtesy of answering their questions, don't you?"

I grimaced. "I guess so."

"Don't frown—you'll ruin your makeup." Olivia patted my arm. "You can do this, Chloe. Just be yourself."

I nodded, but inside I was dying. Olivia had no idea just how "myself" I was about to be!

The assistant hustled over to me. "Nice to see you again, Mrs. Windsor. Are you ready?"

Feeling sick, I nodded.

"You look perfect, as usual." She clipped a small microphone to my dress. "We're going to go ahead and get started. You know the drill—just follow me." She brought me to a high, long table that faced several screens. I remembered the set-up: there was the New York studio, the two attractive hosts facing the cameras. Behind them was a large window that showed the live-NYC audience smiling and waving from the sidewalk.

"Let's go, everyone!" The assistant checked her clipboard and hustled next to the cameraman. Olivia Jensen waved and smiled at me, my redheaded cheerleader.

The lights dimmed as they counted down. "Five, four, three, two..."

"Our next guest is a surprise. So...surprise!" One of

the pretty hosts said. "She's someone we've had on the show recently, and we *loved* talking to her. Hoo boy, this is going to be good. Joining us again is Chloe Windsor, wife of billionaire Bryce Windsor! Can you believe it?"

The second host turned to her. "I am so thrilled that Chloe wanted to talk with us again! I loved having her on a few weeks ago. So much has happened, hasn't it? The Windsor family's been in the news a *lot*. First of all, Gene Windsor, CEO of Windsor Enterprises, was arrested and formally charged." They showed an image of Gene being taken away in handcuffs and wearing his Gucci loafers, of course.

I braced myself, knowing what was coming next.

Host Number One arched her expertly groomed eyebrows. "And it's not the only scandal that's rocked the family lately. Our next guest *also* got into a smack-down with the American heiress Felicia Jones at a high-society wedding. We've obtained an exclusive video—watch this." They showed a video of me wearing that provocative red jumpsuit, jumping on Felicia and pummeling her.

Ugh, I hadn't known someone got it on film...

I saw Olivia's shoulders slump. She hadn't known, either.

The shot returned to the hosts; they both looked like

their eyeballs might pop out. "That's something," Host Number Two said.

The first host nodded in agreement. "I can't picture sweet Chloe doing something like that—so let's bring her on and ask her. Please give our next guest, Chloe Windsor, a warm welcome!"

I longed for the floor to open up and swallow me whole, but alas, I just stood there until my image appeared on the screen. Thank God for Midge and her makeup brush because I looked a hell of a lot better than I felt.

"Hey there, Chloe!" The hosts smiled at me. "That was some introduction, huh?"

"Yeah. It was really something." My palms started to sweat.

"Can we start off by talking about the wedding?" The first host asked gently. "What happened with Felicia Jones? I know there were rumors your husband was cheating on you with her—"

"And those rumors were totally false," a male voice boomed. Bryce strode into the media room, past the stunned production assistant and an openly gaping Olivia Jensen, and joined me at the table.

"Hi, Chloe." He kissed my cheek, then turned to face the cameras.

"Can you two hear me?"

The hosts blinked at him. "Yes, Mr. Windsor—Bryce —we can hear you through Chloe's microphone."

"Perfect." Bryce gave them a wide smile. He looked achingly handsome—with his hair pushed back from his face, a light beard, and his striking navy suit. "I thought I should join you this morning to address some of these concerns. I never do interviews like this, but you two were nice to my wife before--I thought I would return the favor."

The hosts looked as if they might start fanning themselves. Not only was Bryce super hot, but their ratings were going to be on fire! "Please, tell us *everything*. How're you holding up since your father was arrested?"

"I'll get to that in a moment." He put his arm protectively around me. "First things first. My wife was encouraged to get into a fight with Felicia Jones by my father. He's the one who was behind that; Chloe would never act that way. Although in my opinion, Felicia certainly deserved it."

The hosts almost fell out of their respective chairs. "What do you mean? Why did she deserve it? What does your father have to do with it?"

"Felicia and I dated about a million years ago. She cheated on me and broke off our engagement. It took me a long time to get over it, but I did—and I'm so happy." He squeezed me tight. "But Felicia didn't like it when I finally moved on, so she was texting me and being very inappropriate. If you ask me, any woman who tries to steal someone else's husband certainly deserves a bitch slap—if not more. Am I right?"

The hosts were practically fist-pumping. "Yes!"

"You tell it, Bryce!"

"But it was my father that orchestrated that fight. He was blackmailing Chloe. He's never approved of her because she's from a different background. He forced her to do that so she looked bad in the press—he wanted us to separate."

The hosts nodded, eating up every one of my handsome husband's words.

"And that's why we're here. Chloe is so brave. She offered to do this interview by herself and take all the scrutiny. She's so selfless, she wanted to protect me and my position with the company. But she shouldn't have to face this alone. I'm proud of my wife and the life we're building together." Bryce smiled at the cameras. "And that's why I'm here."

He turned to me. "Are you ready to tell them the truth, babe?"

I nodded. I was petrified, but I could face anything as long as Bryce was by my side.

I took a deep, shaky breath. And then I started telling the truth.

"I didn't meet my husband at Dunkin' Donuts. It started a little differently than that..."

We told them everything. On national television. In broad daylight. About the escort agency, Bryce's father's blackmail, the fact that he was the newly appointed CEO of Windsor Enterprises, all of it.

The best part of the interview was the end.

"What do you want to say to your father?" The host asked Bryce.

He squeezed me against him as he considered it.

"Ah, I know." He grinned. "By the way, Dad, congratulations. You're going to be a grandpa!"

The network told us later that our episode was the most watched (and re-watched) in the show's history. The hosts even sent us a gift basket, replete with a silver Tiffany's baby rattle, a bottle of non-alcoholic champagne, and some sort of aromatherapy candle that was supposed to emotionally support you through the first trimester. I lit it, and it smelled great!

Not only was the candle lovely, doing the show had

been a blessing. Telling the truth about my background had been scary. I was embarrassed for Bryce and Noah, but they both said they were fine. Bryce didn't get fired. There was an uproar in the press, but that was the thing about telling the truth. Once it was out, there was no dirt left to dig.

In the end, it was like my mother said: sunlight *was* the best disinfectant. Thank goodness.

For his part, Gene didn't take the news very well. He sent me several more menacing text messages, including phrases like *How dare you, don't you know who I am,* and *you'll pay for this* until Bryce took control and made arrangements to speak with him on the phone.

He put him on speakerphone so I could hear.

"Dad?"

"I can't believe what you've done, legal's going to undo *everything*, and then you'll be out on the streets—"

"No, I won't. You're being prosecuted for other things, too, like violating your fiduciary duty to the company." Bryce smirked. "Regina Hernandez is making a list and checking it twice."

"Son..." Gene sounded so enraged that I could picture blood vessels popping from his forehead. "You have no right to dismantle everything I've worked for. I built my company from the ground up. I don't deserve to be treated like this!"

"I'm going to respectfully disagree with you on that.

I know you had plans to have Noah abducted. What were you thinking? I can't believe that you'd do that. That's a whole level lower than I thought you were capable of."

"I was desperate. You wouldn't break things off with your wife, and she was going to make us all look like trash. And that's exactly what's happened. I can't believe you married an escort!"

"The thing is, she was never really an escort. She was just broke and scared and needed the money to protect her family. But you never looked below the surface, and that's your loss. I hope you rot in there, Dad. With all the additional charges, you won't ever get out of jail again. Have fun! Hope you make some nice friends. I hear the food is great!"

He hung up and put his face in his hands. "I'm sorry you had to hear that."

I nudged him. "I'm sorry you had to be related to that."

"Ha," Bryce said, me too."

Bryce turned to me. "I have a surprise for you." He grinned at me. "Remember I told you about that shower bench in Beacon Hill, Mrs. Windsor?"

I grinned back. "How could I forget?"

He picked me up and cradled me against his massive chest. "You won't ever forget it after tonight! I had one installed in Maine."

I laughed. "When the heck did you have time to do that?"

He waggled his eyebrows. "I'm on billionaire time, babe. And it's always billionaire time."

"It's good to be you, huh?"

He nuzzled his scruff against my neck. "It *is* good."

I had to agree with him on that.

epilogue

CHLOE

"I TOLD YOU, don't put the sand in your mouth. C'mon!" Colby groaned as his youngest, Austin, crammed more mud into his mouth.

"I think he thinks it tastes good." Bryce laughed, but then he looked a little disgusted as Austin happily swallowed.

"Aw, you're gonna get sick, and Mom's gonna be so upset—"

"What's Mom going to be upset about?" Tate hustled down the beach, baby on her hip. Her long blond hair flew out behind her. She and Colby had two kids under three, the youngest of which was only three months, but her body had already returned to rockin' status.

She cursed when she saw her son, mud dribbling down his face. "Austin Jake! Mommy told you no more mud!"

"He's going to rub off on Penelope," Daphne complained to me under her breath. She held Penelope, her little princess, by the hand as we watched Austin digest more sand. "Mommy says no-no to that. Okay, angel?"

Penelope looked up at her, eyes wide, and nodded. The little girl was an angel, well-behaved, studious, and quiet—nothing like her mother!

"Kowabunga!" Noah ran past us with my oldest on his back, James, and they splashed into the freezing Maine water. Boss, who was now fully grown, chased after them happily. Both James and Noah shrieked as the cold surf engulfed them. My youngest, Hazel, reached out toward the water, indicating she wanted to go in. "Not so fast, young lady," I joked. "Mommy would have to carry you in there, and Mommy doesn't want to freeze to death!"

Jake had called that morning from Dubai. He was currently Vice President of Global Initiatives for Windsor Enterprises, and he'd been traveling all over the world. He loved every second of it. Still single, Jake enjoyed being a doting uncle. He especially enjoyed it when he missed things like his nephew Austin ingesting a large quantity of Maine beach sand!

Life was good on the island. Bryce was still CEO, and Windsor Enterprises had flourished under his leadership.

Hazel and Midge were still with us, as was the rest of the staff. Hazel had finally gone on vacation; she'd cried happy tears when Bryce told her we were naming our daughter after her. Midge was as feisty as ever. Bryce had put her niece through school, and now Midge was considering going herself. But I told her I couldn't live without her!

Plus, I'd had my suspicions for some time that she was dating Chef. No confirmation as of yet, but I was working on it!

Mimi and Michael Jones were, somewhat inexplicably, still together. We saw them occasionally at the Nguyen's summer soirées. Mimi had quit drinking. She still held a grudge against me and of course Daphne, but we offered to host her gardening club from time to time, and we never revoked her pool-club membership. What could I say? I was doing my best.

Felicia Jones had married Finn Ryder, but then she'd cheated on him with his drummer. Mimi had been nicer to me after that.

As for the rest of the crew, Akira and Elena were both making bank. Akira had been hired by Jim Wright and had just been named partner at Kellogg, Kramer and Wright LLP. After I'd gone public with my story, Tate had shared hers. Elena's business had grown over one-thousand percent. She was now considered the Queen of the Arranged Marriage, and everyone was flocking to Accommodating.

Both of her girls had graduated from private schools. Elena had even told them she'd pay for grad school!

My dad and Lydia had relocated to sunny Florida. That had been Bryce's idea. Lydia often posted on social media, showing off her lion tattoo as she and my dad strolled the beach. They were still gambling, drinking, and complaining. At least they were far away! They'd wanted a mansion; we'd bought them a nice condo. They'd wanted a Hummer; we'd bought them a truck. It was as close to justice as I was going to get, and I'd made my peace with it.

Bryce ambled over to me, kissed Hazel on the top of her head, and grinned at us. "Hi there, Mrs. Windsor." He put his arm around me.

His touch lit me up from within, the same way it always had.

"Hi yourself." I grinned up at him.

"Will you two get a room?" Daphne joked. She was still married to Gene, happy as a clam that he was spending the rest of his life in prison, and she got to live in all of his mansions and raise her beautiful daughter on her own. She'd also recently gotten back on social media and was selling more shakes than ever!

"Of course we will. As soon as it's nap time." Bryce beamed down at me, and I beamed up at him.

I wasn't even ashamed of how much I loved my husband.

That was him.

That was me.

That was us, and we... We were forever.

Thank you so much for reading this trilogy! It means everything to me. If you enjoyed the story, you will also LOVE my new billionaire club series! It's called *Club 444* and it's a sexy, fast-paced ride that will give you ALL the feels!

Here's the link: www.amazon.com

about the author

USA Today and Amazon Top-10 Bestselling Author Leigh James is currently sitting on a white-sand beach, watching the sunset, dreaming up her next billionaire. Get ready, he's going to be a HOT one!

Just kidding! Leigh is actually freezing her butt off in Maine, USA, where she lives with her awesome husband, their great kids, and her BFF Choco the choco-late lab. But she promises that billionaire is REALLY going to be something!

Leigh also writes Young Adult Paranormal Romance as Leigh Walker. Her smash-hit series *Vampire Royals* was previously optioned by Netflix. Her books have been translated into German, French, Italian, and Portuguese.

Thank you for reading. Lots of love to all of you!

also by leigh james

The Escort Collection

Escorting the Player

Escorting the Billionaire

Escorting the Groom

Escorting the Actress

Escorting the Royal

Jenny and Cole's Story

The Billionaire and I (Book One)

The Billionaire's Hire (Book Two)

The Forever Trilogy

The Forever Contract (Book 1)

The Forever Promise (Book 2)

The Forever Vow (Book 3)

~

Club 444

Worthy Book 1

Worthy Book 2

Worthy Book 3

~

Hot Fake Date

~

Acadia Falls

~

Silicon Valley Billionaires

Book 1

Book 2

Book 3

~

The Liberty Series

sneak peek - escorting the billionaire!

If you enjoyed this book, you might also like my USA Today Bestseller, **Escorting the Billionaire**! Here's the first chapter. Thank you so much for reading!

CHAPTER ONE - JAMES

All I wanted was a date for my stupid asshole brother's wedding.

Not a girlfriend. Not a relationship. A *date*.

No strings. No ties. No games.

No sex.

So when I called Elena at the escort service, I was very clear.

"I want someone beautiful. Who can function at high-society events," I said. "She needs to be able to use her silverware properly and to be discreet. I can't have someone who gets drunk and falls down in public. Also, no one who looks cheap. I don't want a lot of makeup and big, fake boobs."

"I don't have any cheap-looking girls, Mr. Preston," Elena said. "Unless the client is into that. Then I have plenty." She laughed.

I waited for her to finish. "I need her to be available for two weeks. I have cocktail parties, lunches, brunches, the rehearsal dinner, then the wedding. And then for some ungodly reason, my brother wants us all to go on his honeymoon to the Caribbean with him. It's going to be the wedding from hell."

I sighed and rubbed my temples; two weeks with my family was going to be bad enough. And now I was going to have to babysit a hooker the whole time.

But it was better than going alone. I hoped.

"She'll need a passport. And a drug test. I don't want any users." I winced, remembering the last time I'd hired an escort. It had been over ten years ago, but I still clearly remembered waking up and finding her in the bathroom, shooting up in between her toes.

I went on a penicillin and no-whore diet after that.

"All my girls are drug tested," Elena said smoothly, "and they all have passports. They have to travel frequently. It's not a problem." She paused for a beat.

"Speaking of tests, you're going to have to be screened for STDs. I'll need those results emailed to me before we make the final arrangements."

"I'm not planning on actually sleeping with her—" I said.

"Excuse me?" Elena asked.

"I don't want to sleep with her," I insisted. "I need her as a buffer from my family."

"Whatever you like," Elena said sweetly. "But she will be young and gorgeous. And completely at your disposal."

I exhaled and stalked around my living room, my footsteps bouncing off the hardwood floors. I was dressed in a suit and ready for work. I looked out at the sun rising over Los Angeles, the light flooding my house. I didn't want to leave here. I had everything I needed, including my favorite leather couch and an enormous flatscreen television, and nothing I didn't, including a prostitute and my family.

I didn't argue with the madam. Still, I had no plans to sleep with the girl I was hiring—I wanted to keep her at arm's length, just like everyone else. I didn't want any messy emotional entanglements. I just needed a fake relationship to keep my family at bay. No more questions about why I was alone, no more wondering or whispers. The whispers that I was gay. Or worse, that I was lonely.

The truth was that I preferred to be alone, left to my own devices. And it was nobody's damn business.

"I'll have my doctor send you the test results. Tomorrow. I need to get this wrapped up—I fly in on Friday, and I need her then." All the events and the wedding were happening in Boston. Then we were all flying to Providenciales together, one big happy family.

Fuck me, I thought. I needed a drink just running through the itinerary in my mind.

"What sort of look do you prefer?" Elena asked. "I gave you the code to look at the girls online..."

"I already did," I said. "They all look decent. Find me one that won't embarrass me. Find me one that's smart. Not some hick. And no strippers. My brother can pick out a stripper from a mile away."

"Do you have a preference for hair color?" She asked. "Build? Anything? Because you're going to be around your family, you'll want it to seem natural."

I thought of my last girlfriend, Logan. She'd had stick-straight blond hair and not an ounce of fat on her toned, lithe body. And she'd been a total, complete, unending pain in my ass.

"Dark hair," I said. "Curvy. I want someone who isn't afraid of a steak. And who looks good in a bikini—

but not *too* good, if you know what I mean. I don't want someone who's going to have their ass hanging out in public. *Tasteful*, Elena. I need classy."

I rubbed my temples again. I was hiring an escort as a date to my brother's wedding. Classy probably wasn't a reasonable request, all things considered.

"I've got that," Elena said confidently. "In fact, I think I have the perfect girl. I'll send you over the contract. Send me that test result and your deposit."

"How much is it, again?" I asked. The fee was astronomical, if I remembered correctly.

"The total for two weeks, including the travel, is two hundred thousand dollars." She paused for a beat. "Half paid up front. And we're cash-only."

"Don't you think your services are a bit, umm...overpriced?" I asked. "I'm not prepared to pay investment prices for a rented date."

"You're paying for a luxury product," Elena said, not missing a beat. She'd heard this a thousand times from rich men who doubled as cheap bastards.

"The cost breakdown, per hour, is five hundred and ninety-five dollars. You pay your lawyer more than that, I'm sure. And he doesn't always bend over when you tell him to."

If I'd been capable of it, I'd be mildly chastened by that. I let her continue.

"That being said," Elena continued, "the price I'm charging you is our standard rate. I'm not gouging you just because you're a gazillionaire. But *do* feel free to tip generously at the end of your arrangement."

I snorted.

"Your escort is going to be the most beautiful woman you've ever met. She's going to fulfill your every fantasy—which in your case, is being the perfect date for your brother's wedding. If you had any other fantasies"—she paused for effect—"she could fulfill those, too." She laughed again. "But of course, you're not interested in that."

"Ha ha," I said. "For that price, I might just *have* to fuck her." *Six ways from Sunday.* I made myself stop from forming a mental picture.

"Of course," she said. "And once you get a taste, you'll really understand why you're getting your money's worth. By the way—all of our escorts are on birth control. We test them regularly to make sure they're in compliance. So condoms are optional. Her test results are part of the contract. We guarantee healthy, clean girls. So if you're clean, too, you can both relax and just enjoy each other."

She paused and I squirmed, my cock stiffening at her words. It had been a long time.

Down boy, I thought.

"We'll see you soon, Mr. Preston. I'm looking forward to working with you."

We hung up and I shook my head, laughing to myself a little. Two hundred thousand dollars. But the promise in her words would make any man's dick hard. That was the point. That was why Elena's escort service was the most successful, the most exclusive one on the East Coast. She was good at sales.

And based on the pictures she'd sent me, her employees *were* pretty hot.

I willed the stirring of my erection to go away. I was using Elena's service because I was in a bind, not because I couldn't get laid. I needed the perfect woman to bring to my brother's perfect wedding.

So that everybody would leave me the fuck alone.

I hope you enjoyed the first chapter! To keep reading, click here:

Escorting the Billionaire

Thank you!

xxoo

Leigh

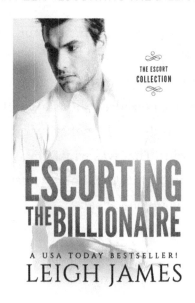

Made in the USA
Las Vegas, NV
15 September 2024

95297670R00163